"You think Jeremy's dating material?" Jessica asked, her voice carefully neutral.

"Most definitely." Jade had a dreamy look on her face. "Cute, sweet . . . and he's got an amazing body, right?"

"Uh, right." Jessica's heart started racing. "Not *that* amazing, though," she added just to be on the safe side. No way she wanted Jade to get the slightest idea she still found him attractive.

Jade pushed a lock of straight, black hair out of her face. "If he doesn't ask me out soon, I'm asking him."

Jessica felt her face go slack and all the color rush from her cheeks. There was no way Jade had just said that.

"You wouldn't care if Jeremy and I went out, would you?" Jade added.

Somehow Jessica forced out a laugh, but it sounded more like she was choking.

"Why would I care?" she blurted out. "He's single. As far as I know anyway." She shrugged, hoping she looked just slightly bored. "We're not that close anymore."

Jade's lips turned up in a sarcastic sort of smile. "That's good because I'd probably date him anyway."

Don't miss any of the books in SWEET VALLEY HIGH
SENIOR YEAR, an exciting series from Bantam Books!

Visit the Official Sweet Valley Web Site on the Internet at:

http://www.sweetvalley.com

Francine Pascal's SVH senior year

As If I Care

CREATED BY
FRANCINE PASCAL

BANTAM BOOKS
NEW YORK · TORONTO · LONDON · SYDNEY · AUCKLAND

RL: 6, AGES 012 AND UP

AS IF I CARE

A Bantam Book / June 2000

Produced by 17th Street Productions,
an Alloy Online, Inc. company.
33 West 17th Street
New York, NY 10011.

ISBN: 0-553-49317-5

Visit us on the Web! www.randomhouse.com/teens

Published simultaneously in the United States and Canada

PRINTED IN THE UNITED STATES OF AMERICA

OPM   0 9 8 7 6 5 4 3 2 1

To Frances & Lucia

Conner McDermott

Women. Can't live with 'em . . .
End of story.

I could do without a part-time
mother who's decided it's time to play
mommy again. And girlfriends. Girlfriends
are definitely not good. That goes for the
girl<u>friends</u> too. Too many expectations.

Definitely too much grief.

Jeremy Aames

Women want mystery. They drool over complicated guys. And I am just not that complicated. So sue me.

So I always try to do the right thing. Does that make me boring? So I get good grades. So I don't blow off assignments. So I show up to work when I say I'm going to. So what? Can't a guy live with his responsibilities and still be cool?

Okay, I'm thinking not.

So I'm boring.

But I'm not going to stay that way.

Ken Matthews

Women are making my life hell. Well, okay, it's not really the women. It's the way my dad treats them. Like slime, only lower.

Dad, I mean, not the women.

Andy Marsden

Women and men.
Men and women.
Men and men.
To tell or not to tell?
Well, that's not really the question, is it?
Am I gay? Am I not? And does anyone really
care? I mean, I'd like to think my <u>friends</u>
would actually care, but the way their lives
are going, forget it. It's always,
  "Andy, what do you think about this?"
  "Andy, I've got a problem."
  "Andy, man, my love life stinks. . . ."
And <u>these</u> are the people I'm counting on?
Pathetic.

CHAPTER 1

Big Deal

From the moment the alarm clock woke him to a splitting headache on Wednesday morning, Conner McDermott had a feeling his day was going to dive straight down the toilet. Driving into the Sweet Valley High parking lot confirmed it. Tia Ramirez's car was already there.

He banged his fist on the steering wheel and immediately winced at the pain the blow sent through his aching head. He'd been hoping to get there before she did so he could slide into their homeroom, bury his face in a book, and avoid her. Now he was going to have to try to hide from her in the halls.

He knew Tia. She'd be waiting to talk to him. That would be talk as in a serious, soul-searching dissection of every little nuance of what happened last night.

As if it was some sort of big deal.

He parked his vintage Mustang and then shook a couple of aspirin out of the bottle in his coat pocket. Why hadn't he dragged his sorry butt out of bed twenty minutes sooner? He hadn't downed *that* much scotch last night, had he? He swallowed the aspirin dry, coughing as the pills stuck halfway down his throat.

Determined to ignore the pain in his head, he grabbed his backpack, slammed the car door, and stalked toward SVH. It was *not* a big deal. It was not a deal at all. So they kissed—so what?

So it was a lot of kissing.

So they were supposed to be best friends.

So he was supposed to be going out with Elizabeth.

He squeezed his way into the building with all the other students and stopped just inside the doorway. Where was Tia? The sea of bodies milling through the halls reminded him of a colony of frantic ants. If she was there waiting for him, he couldn't see her.

He pushed through the crowd toward his locker, keeping his head down. No, they definitely had nothing to talk about. He didn't even know why he had kissed her. No clue at all.

Could have been the scotch, although he could have sworn he'd taken only a couple of swigs. No. He'd kissed her just because he'd damn well felt like it at the moment. He ran a hand over the stubble on his jaw. Actually, knowing him, he'd kissed her because he couldn't resist screwing things up whenever his life looked like it was in danger of actually going well.

But why had Tia kissed him back?

The question made him freeze right in the middle of the hall. Latecomers jostled him as they rushed past. He might have started it, but she had kissed him back. She had most definitely kissed him back.

Conner's stomach tightened until he wondered if he was actually going to heave. She didn't *like* him, as in boy-girl, dating relationship, did she?

Not okay, his pounding brain screamed at him. *That would definitely* not *be okay.*

His backpack slid off his shoulder. As he went to raise it, he noticed a knot of round-faced freshman girls staring at him with wide eyes. He glared at them.

"You're gonna be late," he snapped. They jumped back like a flock of startled pigeons and scattered into the crowd.

As he neared his locker, he caught a glimpse of Elizabeth threading her way toward him, and his heart seized up. What was she doing here? Her homeroom was on the other side of the school.

A horrible thought flashed through his mind, and he really did want to throw up.

Had Tia told her?

Oh God. Please, don't let Tia have told her.

He studied Elizabeth's face but couldn't read anything out of the ordinary. She wasn't smiling, but then again, she didn't look like she was in a huge hurry to claw his eyes out either. In fact, she looked like her normal, put-together self.

Like something really sweet and innocent, he thought. Or maybe it was just the way her pink baby tee made her eyes look so big and blue.

She stopped a few feet away from him and smiled. "Hey, there."

Conner tilted his head slightly and tried to act casual. "Hey."

She opened her mouth to say something but then paused and frowned up at him. "You look kind of pale. Are you okay?"

Conner ran a hand through his hair. *No big deal,* he thought. *Just a hangover. Oh, and I made out with Tia last night.*

Again.

He shook his head. "Just a headache."

"Need some aspirin?"

Conner patted the pocket of his jacket that was packed with pills. "I'm good. What's up?" he made himself ask.

"I just thought we should talk."

His expression must have looked grim because she laid a hand on his forearm. "It's not anything bad. We . . . I just need to talk to you about some stuff, that's all."

Her level tone reassured him. Not even Elizabeth would be this calm if she wanted to talk about what a two-timing bastard he was.

4

He nodded. "Sure. Anytime you want."

"Great." She glanced up at the ceiling. "Let's see. I don't have to be at the *Oracle*—"

The bell interrupted her, and Elizabeth jumped. "Shoot. We're late. I'll talk to you about this later." She stood there awkwardly for a moment, as if she wasn't sure what to do. Conner wondered if she was thinking the same thing he was—that they sometimes used to kiss when they parted and it felt odd not to.

Finally Elizabeth shot him a tight smile and rushed off down the hall.

Conner watched her go, barely able to breathe. So she hadn't kissed him, but she hadn't kicked him in the shin either. At this point Conner had to be grateful for the small things.

He shuffled toward his locker. The hall was quickly emptying, but a flash of bright color caught his eye.

It was Tia.

She was standing directly across the hall. Alone. The instant they made eye contact, she took off. But not before Conner had a good look at the pained expression in her eyes.

Great.

It took him about half a second to decide to skip homeroom. No way he was going to face her now. No way in hell. He grabbed his books for first period out of his locker, slammed it shut, and headed back out toward the parking lot.

*   *   *

I could really hate her, Jessica Wakefield thought as she watched her supposed friend, Jade Wu, slip into first-period history just ahead of her.

No one but Jade would dare wear a crinkled gauze shirt and a long, crinkly gauze skirt together. On anybody else, it would look like a costume for a tacky seventies theme party. On Jade, it worked. In fact, it looked great.

Eric Price pushed right past Jessica without saying a word. He touched Jade's arm, causing her to turn around. "Hey, Jade," he said in this stupid, eager voice. "Cool outfit."

Jade grinned up at him appreciatively. "Thanks, Eric." He ducked his head and shuffled off to his seat, his cheeks bright red.

Jessica rolled her eyes.

"Hi, Jess," Jade said, smirking in her direction.

"Hi." Jessica gave her a big, fake smile. She was surprised Jade was even talking to her after the confrontation they'd had the night before. How irritating that Jade had chosen to take the high road.

Jessica hurried to her seat across the aisle and took a deep breath. So Jade looked completely adorable—so what? She *always* looked adorable. Which probably had something to do with the fact that Jessica's ex-boyfriend couldn't keep his eyes off Jade.

Ever since the girl started working at House of Java, Jeremy had been flirting with her in front of

Jessica. If you could call the lame attempts at conversation Jeremy started flirting. Still, it looked like Jade was eating up the attention.

Not that Jessica cared.

She grabbed her textbook out of her messenger bag and almost slammed it down on the desk. Okay, so she did care. And it was driving her completely insane. Why should she be annoyed about her ex-boyfriend being interested in Jade? *She* was the one who dumped Jeremy. *She* was the one who decided she didn't want him.

But what if Jade did?

Jade's gaze flickered over Jessica's new striped tee.

"Nice shirt," she commented. "I wouldn't have pictured you in those colors. But it works on you. Really," she added after just the slightest hesitation.

Oh, very *convincing,* Jessica thought. But she made herself smile anyway. "Thanks."

While Jade opened her notebook, Jessica glanced furtively at the yellow and purple stripes of her shirt. Jade probably thought she looked ridiculous and just wanted Jessica to wear the shirt to work so Jeremy would see it.

Jessica plopped into her seat. She couldn't take much more of this. And if Jade and Jeremy started dating, it would be ten thousand times worse. Right now it was just irritating, but if she had to put up with gross public displays of affection, she was going to lose it.

The thought of Jade and Jeremy kissing made her sick to her stomach. She pictured herself walking in on them in the back room, seeing them plastered all over each other. Jade would give her a smug look, and Jeremy would . . . who knew how he'd handle it? Jessica sure didn't want to find out.

Mr. Crowley was scrawling something about the War of 1812 on the board. Jessica sighed and flipped open her binder. She traced her pen up and down the pink line on the edge of the notebook paper. No doubt about it, having to work with Jeremy and Jade as a couple would be worse than living in a war zone.

Unfortunately, the only way to convince herself she was worrying about nothing was to ask. Not directly, of course. The last thing in the world she wanted to do was give Jade any ammunition.

Or let it get back to Jeremy that she even slightly cared.

The bell rang. While Mr. Crowley called the roll, Jessica leaned across the aisle toward Jade. She pointed at Bruce Mullins, who was sitting in the front row. "That greasy-hair look is *not* happening," she whispered.

Jade grinned back. "Tell me about it."

"I'm so glad Brian Cogley doesn't do that anymore. He's really gotten cuter this year, don't you think?"

"Definitely." Jade was copying something off the

board as she talked. "He's done a total turnaround since he made the football team."

"I know. Totally." Jessica sketched a cannon in the margin of her notes. "He'd be on a list of datable guys."

Jade continued to write. "Sure."

Calm and cool, Jessica coached herself. She heaved a fake sigh. "I'm kind of disappointed in House of Java. After all those grown-up health freaks I saw when I worked at Healthy, I thought I'd meet more datable guys working at a coffeehouse."

Jade pulled the band out of her glossy, black hair. Her dark eyes were unreadable. "Lots of the guys that come in are datable, just taken. Don't you think?"

"True." Jessica shrugged. "And it's not like our staff's so big."

"Yeah, and you've already gone out with the only decent guy there." Jessica could have sworn Jade smirked at her again. "Tough luck."

Jessica took her time drawing a cannonball blasting across the page. "You think Jeremy's dating material?" she asked, her voice carefully neutral.

"Most definitely." Jade had a dreamy look on her face. "Cute, sweet . . . and he's got an amazing body, right?"

"Uh, right." Jessica's heart started racing. "Not *that* amazing, though," she added just to be on the safe side. No way she wanted Jade to get the slightest idea she still found him attractive.

Jade pushed a lock of straight, black hair out of her face. "If he doesn't ask me out soon, I'm asking him."

Jessica felt her face go slack and all the color rush from her cheeks. There was no way Jade had just said that.

"You wouldn't care if Jeremy and I went out, would you?" Jade added.

Somehow Jessica forced out a laugh, but it sounded more like she was choking.

"Why would I care?" she blurted out. "He's single. As far as I know anyway." She shrugged, hoping she looked just slightly bored. "We're not that close anymore."

Jade's lips turned up in a sarcastic sort of smile. "That's good because I'd probably date him anyway."

"What?" Jessica whispered before she could stop herself. Then she quickly flipped her hair back off her shoulder and turned her attention toward the teacher, trying to cover. "Whatever."

Another great friend, Jessica thought. Why did she always end up with back-stabbing girls who were only out for themselves?

Suddenly Jade reached across the aisle and patted Jessica's arm. "I was just kidding."

Jessica glanced at her. How could Jade manage to sound completely sincere and still have this look like she was laughing at Jessica behind her back?

Mr. Crowley was mumbling something about a British invasion. Jessica stared at Jade's profile as the other girl started taking notes. Something told her Jade wasn't even remotely kidding.

She jotted down a note in the margin of her book.

Personal rule #24:

All's fair in love and war.

She had no idea how it had happened, but this situation was about to turn into one big, fat war.

By the time he made it to third period, Conner knew without a doubt his nightmare of a day was going to keep getting worse. It wasn't enough that the only empty seat in the room was right in the front row, but it was also the seat next to Maria Slater. The girl was nosier than a country-club gossip.

Conner flopped into the chair and opened his notebook, hoping that if he looked productive, his teacher wouldn't ask him anything.

"So, let's go over the homework," Mr. Hauptman said, clasping his hands like he did every day. Conner shrank down in his seat a bit as the overly large man hovered right in front of his desk. Maybe if he wished hard enough, Conner could just disappear.

"Mr. McDermott?"

No such luck.

"Why don't you come up to the board and copy out the first homework problem?" There was an unmistakable edge of amusement in the man's voice.

It was at that exact moment that Conner realized if he was going to blow off assignments, he'd better at least come up with good excuses.

Time froze. Mr. Hauptman picked up a piece of chalk and tossed it up and down in one hand, waiting. Conner could feel all the other students looking at him. Maria had a puzzled and smug expression on her face. And she was supposed to be his friend. Sort of.

Think fast, McDermott.

Nothing. His brain switched off as if he'd blown a power circuit.

"Mr. McDermott?" the teacher prompted.

Conner cleared his throat and sat up straight in his chair. "I left it in my locker," he mumbled.

"No problem." Mr. Hauptman stepped aside and motioned to Conner to approach the board. "Since we only had three problems last night, I'll bet you remember most of it, right? Let's see how far you can get."

Conner stared down at the blank page in his notebook. Busted. He hadn't even started reading the chapter. He'd been too busy being angry, getting drunk, seducing Tia. Conner swallowed hard. He doubted he could even write out the problem correctly, let alone get through the first step.

He just gazed at Mr. Hauptman. It was obvious the guy knew that Conner was clueless. How long was he going to let this torturous battle of wills endure?

Finally the teacher sighed and crossed his arms over his round belly. He gave Conner a sharp look over the tops of his reading glasses.

"A word of advice, Mr. McDermott. Next time you might want to try an amusing anecdote. Something involving an alien abduction might be more believable."

The whole class erupted in laughter.

Of course he'd have to insult Conner first. No surprise there. Much to his disappointment, Conner felt his cheeks start to burn. He slunk down as far as he could until his knees were wedged up against the bottom of the desk. And he needed this crap why?

Across the aisle Maria leaned forward in her seat to get his attention. She shot him one of those what's-the-matter-are-you-okay? sympathy looks.

Was that supposed to make him feel better?

Actually, it was better than the other looks she'd been giving him lately. The you-hurt-my-best-friend-and-you-die look and the I-always-knew-you-were-worthless-scum look. Still, sympathy was not what he needed right now.

What he needed was more aspirin and a copy of the homework.

A swig of whiskey wouldn't hurt either.

Jessica Wakefield

Many things are said over the next few days, but don't get drawn back into the mess. What's done is done. Leave it that way.

CHAPTER 2

Good Advice Givers

As Tia pulled her mother's car up to the curb by the park down the street from school, Andy picked up the brown paper bag at his feet and eyed the snacks and drinks inside. He grinned over at her when he saw her selection of goodies.

"My idea of the perfect lunch," he said. "Thanks for buying."

Tia smiled and pulled her hair back into a bright blue rubber band that perfectly matched the color of her shirt.

"You're welcome," she answered. "Thanks for keeping me company. I could use it today."

"Me too." He pulled out a package of chocolate cupcakes and squinted at the label. "I think I read somewhere that these were designed to be edible for years in the event of a nuclear disaster."

"That's great." Tia rolled her eyes. "Just what I look for in junk food. Something that will stay on the hips forever."

Andy ran a finger across the crinkly plastic. He gave Tia a sidelong glance, then focused his attention on a palm tree just outside the windshield.

"Not that I don't appreciate free food, but why the lunch invitation?"

Tia didn't hesitate. "The truth is, I can't handle being around Conner and Liz today," she said in a confidential tone. "And I need some advice."

Andy had to concentrate to keep from sighing out loud. It seemed like all they ever talked about anymore was Conner and Elizabeth.

"Okay," he said, leaning back in his seat. "But then you have to return the favor. I could use a little perspective myself." The last time he'd tried to talk to Tia about his own issues, he hadn't gotten a word in edgewise. Maybe he'd have better luck this time.

"Great," Tia said with a halfhearted grin. "We can play Ann Landers for each other."

Andy grimaced reflexively. "Not her. She's way too chipper. I prefer Jerry Springer, but I'll take what I can get as long as it comes with cupcakes and soda."

Tia laughed. "And chips," she added, rolling down her window and letting in a breeze of fresh air. "That's better," she said, taking a deep breath.

Andy handed Tia a diet soda and a bag of corn chips. "Yeah, I mean if we're going to kill ourselves by ingesting this crap, we might as well breathe healthily while we do it," he said. He was actually amazed at the calming effect the breeze had on him. Andy was suddenly more relaxed than he'd been in days. That wasn't saying much, but it was something.

Tia pushed back her seat, ripped open the chips, and ate all of two before she started to look ill. She focused on Andy, her eyes hard and serious. "Swear you won't tell anybody?"

Andy smirked. That was another phrase he'd heard a lot lately. He struggled to open the package of cupcakes and keep from getting annoyed. Tia was still his friend, and she did have legitimate issues. Even if they did spring from her own dumb decisions. "On my honor as a caffeine addict," he said.

She frowned at him. "This is completely serious."

"Then I'll swear completely seriously," he said, finally popping a cupcake out of its little plastic compartment.

Tia picked up a chip and then dropped it back in the bag. "I can't believe this," she said, mostly to herself. She stared down at the gearshift for a long minute. "Conner kissed me again," she said finally. "I mean he kissed me a lot."

Andy froze, a cupcake halfway to his mouth. "And?"

"And I kind of liked it," she answered softly. "That's the bad part."

"Okay, then." He took a bite and chewed for a moment, trying to figure out what he was supposed to say. Not much came to mind other than "how crazy are you?" so he settled on an alternative. "This could be a problem," he said finally.

Tia sighed and took a swig of soda. "I was kind of thinking that."

"Do you and Conner—? I mean, are you and Conner thinking about, you know, going out?"

"No," she answered quickly, wiping her mouth with the back of her hand. "No way. He loves Liz." She leaned back and shoved her fingers into her dark hair. "But . . ."

Andy could see the pain in her brown eyes. "Uh-oh. Here comes the big *but*."

Tia laughed dryly. "You are so lucky, you know? You always have such a clear perspective on things. Andy of the perfect life."

Andy's stomach turned over quickly, and he lowered the second half of the cupcake. "You'd be surprised."

"Oh, that's right," Tia said, pulling one leg up on the car seat and turning to face him. "I'm sorry— you said you needed to talk too." She put her bag of chips aside and settled her hands in her lap. "What's not perfect in your life?"

Andy tossed the rest of his cupcake and the container into the bag at his feet. "Relationships, what else?"

"Yeah?" she asked. "You never did say why you and Six broke up. Is that it?"

"You're getting warm." He stared out the window

at the empty play area. Life had been so nice when he was little and all he'd had to worry about was swinging high and hanging on to the merry-go-round.

"I'm totally confused about this opposite-sex thing, I think." He stopped, then smacked his thigh in frustration. "No, I am. I *am* confused. Completely. I don't think I felt the way I was supposed to when I was with Six. I'm even wondering if I might—"

"I'm confused too," Tia cut in. "I don't feel at all about Conner the way I felt with Angel, and then I worry that I'm never going to feel that way again." She stopped and shook her head. "I'm sorry. You were talking about Six."

"That's okay," he said automatically, although it really wasn't. He never interrupted his friends when they were talking about something important.

But Tia was here now, ready to listen, so he swallowed his frustration. "It's not about Six, not really," Andy went on. "It's about . . ." He traced a heart on the passenger window. "Okay, this is going to sound completely weird, but when we were dating, I felt like I wanted to spend more time around her brother than I did with her."

He tried to study her expression without letting her know he was. To his relief, she didn't look shocked at all. "That doesn't sound weird," she said. "Sometimes I'd rather be with my girlfriends than Angel. He'd get so serious and focused."

Her face lit up, and she sat bolt upright, squishing the bag of chips in her lap. "Hey! Maybe that's what I'm looking for. Maybe that's what this whole thing with Conner is about. I've been with Mr. Serious and Safe for so long, I'm looking for something fun. And maybe dangerous. It's classic. Do you think?"

Andy gritted his teeth. "Only if I have to."

"Oh, come on." Tia gave him a shove. "I'm right, aren't I?"

"Sure," he said with a shrug. *And thanks so much for listening to my little problems.*

Tia popped a chip into her mouth and munched on it happily. "I agree." She let out a big sigh. "It's like knowing why I've been acting like a psycho makes it so much easier to handle. I feel so much better. How about you?"

"Oh, tons."

"See? We're good advice givers." She dusted off her hands and started the car. "We should talk more often."

Andy eyed the barren playground, feeling just as empty as the untouched swings. "No doubt."

Lunch sucked. School sucked. Even the beautiful weather sucked. As Conner headed back into the building to get his books for seventh period, he was pretty sure nothing would ever not suck again.

All through their lunch period Elizabeth had

seemed really distant. As in ready-to-break-up distant. What had happened to her early morning good mood? What had happened to the girl who almost kissed him and wanted to talk to him ASAP?

Was she really being cold to him at lunch, or was he just projecting?

"Dammit," Conner muttered, running a hand through his badly-in-need-of-a-haircut hair. His life was getting ridiculous. He didn't know what was real and what was his guilty conscience playing tricks on him anymore. True, he probably deserved the confusion and irritation. But still, he and Elizabeth hadn't gotten two seconds alone so he could find out what she wanted to tell him. And now he'd have to stress out about it until after school.

"You're not stressed," Conner told himself. He didn't *get* stressed about relationships. It was one of his personal rules.

Unfortunately, it seemed like all of his personal rules were out the window when it came to Elizabeth Wakefield.

He yanked open the courtyard door and stalked into the hall. At least he'd managed to keep away from Tia all day. He hadn't been able to believe his luck when she and Andy had failed to show up at lunch. At least that was one thing he had going for him.

"Conner, wait up."

He whirled around to see Tia slip in the door behind him.

Moron, he chided himself. He should have known better than to think anything was going his way.

"Hey," he called back unenthusiastically. Badly as he wanted to tear off down the hall, he made himself wait for her to catch up. Making a break for it now would be the lamest of lame moves.

Tia was breathing hard by the time she skidded to a stop next to him. For the first time in his life Conner found that he couldn't look her in the eye.

"We need to talk. Soon," she said urgently. "Can you meet me after eighth?"

Conner forced himself to glance at her and almost winced. She looked awful—sad and angry and fragile at the same time.

This was definitely not anything he was ready to handle. Why was it always his responsibility to fix everybody's feelings? So they'd gotten a little physical. So what? Were they supposed to be all deep now?

A tiny part of Conner's conscience reminded him that his relationship with Tia already *was* deep—that it always had been. And that she had every right to expect something more now that they'd given in to the sexual tension.

But that wasn't what Conner wanted to hear. He wanted the whole thing to fade into a distant memory. And it would . . . unless they talked it to death, like she wanted to.

"I can't." Conner's brain raced as he tried to

think of a good excuse. He shoved his hands in the front pockets of his jeans and felt his lucky guitar pick, the one his teacher, Gavin, had given him.

He tried not to smile. "I have a guitar lesson today. Sorry."

Tia narrowed her eyes at him, and Conner froze. "On a Wednesday? Since when? I thought Gavin played I'm-a-big-cool-rock-star with his band on Wednesdays."

She knew him too well. Conner suddenly flashed on a memory from the night before—he and Tia hitting the couch, flopping down awkwardly because they were too busy kissing to look where they were going. Ugh. How could he have *done* that? She was like his sister. Just being near her now was making him want to crawl out of his skin—knowing he'd kissed her that way, touched her that way. It was just wrong.

"Conner?" Tia prompted.

Conner stared down at his scuffed boots. "Look, one of the guys is out of town, and so he asked me if I wanted to change our lesson. He wants to take tomorrow off and spend some time with his girl-friend."

He ran a finger along the hard edge of the pick. If he could just lie low for another couple of days, the whole thing would be old news. Maybe the oddity of it would all fade with time.

Tia crossed her arms over her chest, and Conner knew his confidence was premature.

"You don't believe me?" he asked, his face burning.

"Maybe because you've never strung that many words together in one sentence in your life," she said snottily.

Normally Conner would shoot back something sarcastic, but he suddenly didn't have it in him. Instead he gave her a sincere look. Or at least he hoped it looked sincere. "Today's just really bad. We'll get together," he said.

Tia raised her eyebrows. "Pinky swear?"

Conner rolled his eyes and held up his pinky. "Yes," he said, clenching his teeth. He really couldn't take much more of this.

"Great, so we'll talk." Tia backed slowly away, her books held tight against her chest. "Tomorrow, right?"

Conner nodded and shoved his hands back into his pockets, where they instantly balled into fists. The pick dug into his palm, but he barely noticed. Did he owe her his whole life now? Well, she could just get in line behind everybody else who wanted a piece of him.

And it was a hell of a line.

"Are you gonna eat that?"

Jeremy Aames looked up when he heard the voice of his best friend, Trent, then down at the barely touched sandwich in his hand. Normally he devoured two sandwiches this size at lunch along with a bag of chips, an apple, and a few chocolate-chip cookies, but today he had zero appetite.

"No. You can have it," he said quickly. He tossed the sandwich to Trent over the body of their other friend, Stephanie Mullen, who was stretched out on the grass between them.

"Hey, watch it!" Stephanie warned, checking her stomach for stray pieces of chicken salad.

While Trent wolfed down the rest of Jeremy's lunch, Jeremy stared out over the lawn of Big Mesa High School at the street. He'd been thinking about Jade all morning, trying to talk himself into asking her out. And sometimes trying to talk himself out of it. His goal changed about every five seconds.

Stephanie frowned up at him. "You're looking serious."

Jeremy plucked a blade of grass from the ground and wound it around his index finger. "There's this girl at work I was thinking about asking out."

"What's to think about?" Trent swallowed a huge bite of sandwich. "If you like her . . ."

"I do like her. It's just . . . she's kind of . . . I don't know." He paused. How *would* he describe Jade? Cool? Intense? Outrageous? "Different, I guess," he said finally.

Stephanie and Trent gave him blank looks.

"She's not like the other girls I've gone out with," Jeremy explained. "I don't know. Not . . ."

"Not all cute and peppy," Stephanie finished for him, pushing her black hair back with the aid of her big, Audrey Hepburn sunglasses.

"Right," Jeremy said, embarrassed at how predictable he was. "She's just kind of . . . out there."

Trent grinned and nodded appreciatively, still chewing. "A wild woman, huh?" he said through a mouthful of food.

Jeremy snorted and ripped up some more grass. "Yeah, right."

But when he really thought about it, Jade actually was kind of wild. At least more so than anyone else he'd ever dated. She thought nothing of skipping out on work, she'd held her own against Jessica when they'd argued, and she dressed like a cross between a hippie and a biker chick. She was kind of dangerous, but in a good way.

"She could definitely cause some trouble," Jeremy said, eyeing his friends.

But these days trouble sounded fun.

Anything beyond his boring existence sounded fun.

Trent balled up the sandwich wrap and tossed it into Jeremy's crumpled lunch bag. When his father had gotten a new job and started making some money again, Jeremy had quit brown bagging it . . . for about two seconds—until he tasted the cafeteria food.

"I say, the wilder the better," Trent said. "I mean, go

28

for it, man. You could definitely use some loosening up."

"Yeah," Stephanie added, grabbing a grape from her lunch tray and popping it into her mouth. "It's about time you dated somebody who hasn't made the perfect attendance list since kindergarten."

"You guys, I am not that bad," Jeremy protested.

"Yeah, you are," Trent said, his eyes innocent.

Stephanie nodded. "Oh, definitely." She pointed to his backpack. "Did you finish that calculus work sheet?"

Jeremy eyed her suspiciously. "Yes."

"Ha," she blurted out, throwing up her hands. "It's not even due until next week. You *are* that bad."

Jeremy shredded the blade of grass in his hand, adding the pieces to the little pile in front of him. "Great, so then why am I even thinking about asking out a girl who's going to think I'm a huge dork?" he said, lamenting at how pathetic he sounded. "I don't think she's even into school that much."

Trent leaned back on his elbows and stretched out his long legs. "Because opposites attract," he said.

"And you need a life," Stephanie added.

Trent nodded and closed his eyes as he tilted his face toward the sun. "You definitely need a life."

Jeremy laughed. "Thanks a lot, guys."

"Don't mention it," Trent said. "Just ask her out."

Jeremy brushed the pieces of grass off his legs. "Well, there's one other problem," he said. "She works at House of Java with me."

"So what?" Trent asked, his face scrunching up.

Jeremy's heart thudded. "So what if we go out and things don't work out?" he said, feeling like he was stating the obvious.

Trent shrugged. "So they don't work out." He opened his eyes and flicked his gaze at Jeremy. "Why? You're not thinking she's the stalker type, are ya?"

"I can't see that." Jeremy grinned. In-your-face, self-assured Jade chasing *him* down? Not even.

Stephanie sat up and brushed grass out of her dark hair. "Don't worry about the work thing. I dated that guy George when we both worked at the Gap. It wasn't any big deal."

"But what if something happens?" Jeremy asked quietly. "What if we go out for a while and then break up and then we have to work together?" He already knew all about the consequences. It had happened with Jessica. Weeks of discomfort, followed by days of confusion, followed by hours of awkwardness, followed by more confusion.

"What's the big deal?" Trent asked. "You already did it with Jessica, and you both lived. So things are weird for a couple of days. You deal, and you move on. Jessica did it, and now you're doing it."

Jeremy's stomach turned at the thought of Jessica moving on and who she'd moved on with. He wondered if that would ever go away and if it was normal to still feel that way about a relationship that had been over for weeks.

"Trent's right," Stephanie said, pulling a tube of clear lip gloss out of her bag. "Besides, if things were that bad, you could always work different shifts."

Jeremy looked from Trent to Stephanie. "So, you guys really think I should go for it?"

His friends traded exasperated looks.

"No," Trent said, closing his eyes again and flopping back onto the ground. "We think you should read another chapter of calculus."

Elizabeth Wakefield

Tia's avoiding me. And I think she's avoiding Conner. I've been alternately avoiding Conner and talking to Conner. I think Andy's trying not to avoid anybody, but I get the feeling he really wants to avoid everybody. And Conner's just Conner. Which basically means he may or may not be avoiding everyone. It's so hard to tell.

When did everything get so complicated?

I mean, I told Tia I was going to tell Conner to stay away from her, but I never did. Does she think I did? Is that why she's avoiding him? And if that's why, do I tell her I never told him or do I just be petty and enjoy the fact that they don't seem to be talking?

Because it's awful, but I actually feel

better that they're not talking. If they're not getting close enough to talk, then they're obviously not getting close enough to kiss.

And at the moment that's all I care about.

I guess it's really not that complicated when you think about it.

Conner hunched down in his seat in creative writing and crossed his arms over his chest. Mr. Quigley was in the middle of scribbling another poem on the front board.

"Okay, class," he said when he'd finished. "What's the author's message here?" He glanced around the room. "Anybody?"

Conner slumped farther down until the back of his head rested against the hard plastic of the chair back. He scowled and scribbled in his notebook:

Life is a black pit leading to hell.

Mr. Quigley pointed at Andy. "Mr. Marsden? Any thoughts?"

Andy shook his head. "Nothing worth saying out loud."

The class laughed.

Conner looked over at his friend. Disconnected as he was, he could still see that Andy looked pretty down. Even the guy's red curls seemed to be drooping. Conner knew he should ask what was up, but today he just couldn't handle anybody else's problems.

Andy hunched over his desk, then tore off a scrap of paper and waved it in Conner's direction. Conner waited until the teacher turned his back and then held out his hand. Andy slapped the note into it.

You look unthrilled. What's up?

Conner sighed. Leave it to Andy. The kid was never distracted by his own problems like Conner was. It was almost endearing, but Conner didn't want to get into any self-analysis right now. He leaned over the paper and added his jagged scrawl.

When don't I?

Then he folded the paper in half and tossed it onto Andy's desk.

Andy laughed and crumpled it up, shoving it into his beat-up messenger bag.

"Okay, everyone, here's tonight's assignment," Mr. Quigley said. "And I don't want to see the sorry effort I got from you last time. I know you have brains. Let's try using 'em."

Mr. Quigley walked up and down the aisles,

handing out the assignment sheets. During the break Andy leaned across his desk toward Conner.

"Can I ask you a stupid question?" he said.

Conner shrugged. If this was about Elizabeth or Tia, he was going to have to run screaming from the room.

"Do you fantasize a lot?" Andy whispered.

Conner snorted. Where had *that* come from? "About?" he asked cautiously.

Andy's eyes darted nervously toward the other side of the room, where Quigley had stopped to talk to Maisie Greene. "You know, uh, girls and stuff."

Conner smirked. "Every chance I get."

Andy nodded. He looked totally deflated. "That's what I thought."

Conner shifted in his seat and glanced toward the front of the room at the back of Elizabeth's head. He wondered what she'd think if she knew he spent half his waking hours thinking about her and had never thought about Tia once. At least not in the same way. He took a deep breath and looked back at Andy. He still had that morose expression on his face. Conner sighed.

"Andy, are you feeling okay?" he asked reluctantly.

Andy checked out the students in the seats around them. Then he leaned closer. "Well, actually, not really. I kind of need someone to—"

Suddenly Conner realized exactly what was going

on. He reached out and slapped Andy on the back. "Second thoughts about breaking up with Six, huh? She's a hot girl."

Andy's face was bright red, and he turned his attention to his desk, lining his book up straight with the notepaper under it. "Not exactly. It's just . . . I don't know. . . ." He shrugged, leaving his sentence unfinished.

"Don't stress," Conner advised. "Just ask her out again. Tell her you were confused or something. Girls love that touchy-feely crap."

Andy stabbed his paper with his pen. "I wish."

Mr. Quigley cupped his hands around his mouth so he could be heard over the chatter that had broken out around the room. "All right, people, let's turn in the haiku assignments," he yelled.

Notebooks snapped open, and pages rustled all around Conner. Mr. Quigley glanced at the clock above the door and then held up his hands. "Before you turn them in, we've got a minute to share at least a few of them with the class."

Conner opened his notebook too and pretended to search for the assignment. He drew his brows together and tried to look like he was completely intent on his notes. This whole faking-involvement thing was getting old real fast.

And it also wasn't working in the slightest. Mr. Quigley's voice carried over the classroom noise. "Conner, you never disappoint. Why don't we start with your poem?"

Conner shrugged. What the hell? After getting burned in calculus, he might as well just go for it. He cleared his throat and looked Mr. Quigley straight in the eye. "I didn't do it."

The teacher's eyes widened in surprise, and his mouth drew into a tight, disapproving line. "See me after class," he ordered.

Enid Rollins read her bizarre haiku about frogs, and the bell rang a minute later. Conner took his time gathering his books before approaching Mr. Quigley's desk. He was trying to keep his temper under control. So what if he missed one lousy poetry assignment? Did everybody in the idiot world have to climb all over him today?

He shuffled toward the teacher's desk, his backpack banging against his thigh as he moved between the desks. Mr. Quigley looked up and sighed. Then he rubbed his eyes with one hand. He looked tired. Or maybe just disgusted. Either way, Conner thought it was a bit of an overreaction.

"You know my homework policy, Mr. McDermott," he said finally. "Any missed assignment knocks down your grade."

Conner shrugged.

"I was under the impression you enjoyed creative writing," Mr. Quigley continued. "Do you want to tell me why you're not getting your work done?"

Conner could just feel himself get instantly defensive and angry. Like he really had time for some formulaic poetry with everything else that was going on in his life. He forced himself to answer. "Just didn't get to it."

Mr. Quigley frowned. "That attitude isn't going to cut it in this class. I won't tolerate missing assignments." He stood up and studied Conner's face for a long moment before he continued. "You've got a lot of talent, son, you really do. But being in this class is a privilege, and if you're not willing to work, I'll replace you with another student who is. Understood?"

Conner shrugged again. Where did this guy get off, being so high-and-mighty? He was a lousy high-school teacher.

"I'll give you another chance to get this assignment done, but I'm still going to dock you a grade on it. Get it to me at the beginning of class tomorrow."

"Fine," Conner said through clenched teeth. He turned quickly and stalked out of the room before lecture man could continue his reprimands.

This was getting out of control. He'd had to endure enough guilt at home lately. He didn't need it at school too.

Moments after the last bell rang, Jessica rushed into the locker room to change for cheerleading practice. She was hoping to get in a little stretching on her own before everyone got there, but she had no such luck. Jade was standing in the middle of the room with her foot up on one of the benches so she could tie her shoe.

"Oh, good, it's you," Jade said when she looked up.

"Yeah, it's me," Jessica answered, wondering why Jade would be glad to see her. Jessica was still waiting for a rehash of the confrontation they'd had at HOJ. "Why aren't you changing?" Jessica asked, tossing her SVH duffel bag on the floor in front of her gym locker.

"I need an honest opinion," Jade said, standing up. She smoothed down the front of her skirt. "Does this outfit look okay on me?"

Jessica almost rolled her eyes. The girl *knew* how good she looked. But she held her tongue and pretended to consider the ankle-length gauze skirt. "It's cute."

"It's not too . . . out there?"

Jessica's brow knitted as she looked at her friend. It was *definitely* out there. But that's what Jade always went for. And it always worked.

Jade walked over to the full-length mirror at the end of the row of lockers and turned to the side to check her profile. "I mean, do you think Jeremy would like it?" she asked.

"Oh." Jessica knelt and started to pull her practice clothes out of her bag, trying to keep from making eye contact with Jade. "Sure. I guess so," Jessica said finally, hoping she sounded casual.

Stop it, she told herself, realizing she was acting

like a nervous, jealous little girl. *Jealous*. The word hit her like a blow. This was so annoying. She wasn't supposed to be jealous. She was the one who had dumped Jeremy. She was over him.

Or at least she thought she was.

Jade plucked at the fabric of her skirt and twisted her hips from side to side, making the deep purple fabric brush over her shoe tops. "You think? Because I have to put it back on after practice and go to work."

Jessica let out a long breath. "Yes, he'll like it," she managed to say. "Jeremy's not heavy into image anyway."

"Oh . . . okay," Jade said with a grin. "Sorry for being such a dork." She reached over and grabbed her water bottle. "Bathroom run. I'll be right back," she said.

Jessica sank down on the bench in front of her locker, absently clutching her workout clothes in her fists. Why did it have to be Jade of all girls? Why did it have to be someone she shared half her classes with and cheered with and *worked* with?

"Why Jade?" Jessica muttered aloud.

"Why Jade what?"

Jessica almost jumped out of her skin at the sound of another voice behind her. Her heart rate only calmed down when Lila Fowler rounded the bench and perched next to her. "You scared me," Jessica said, pulling off her T-shirt and yanking her tank top on over her head.

"Sorry," Lila said reaching over to spin her lock. "Why Jade what?"

Jessica paused. She and Lila hadn't talked about anything personal in months. Things had calmed down between them, but it still felt weird. Jessica mentally ran over the Jade-and-Jeremy subject, trying to figure out how Melissa Fox might use it against her if Lila reported back to the girl.

She hated that she had to do that.

"You don't have to tell me," Lila said finally, sounding uncomfortable.

Jessica took a deep breath. What the hell? Lila was asking to be trusted, and this wasn't earth-shattering news by anyone's standards except her own.

"Jeremy likes Jade," she said quickly. "He was, like, all over her the other night at work."

Lila's face scrunched up. "Wait. Jeremy, that hottie from Big Mesa you used to go out with?"

Jessica nodded, and Lila snorted a little laugh, popping open her locker. "I *do not* see those two together," she said, gathering her dark hair back in a high ponytail.

"Thank you!" Jessica said, kicking off her sandals. "It doesn't make sense."

"Totally bizarre. I mean, he's all preppy and smart looking and mature and stuff," Lila said. "The last guy Jade dated had an eyebrow ring and a lizard named Anthrax." Jessica giggled. Sometimes she really missed Lila.

"Wait a second." Lila stopped what she was doing and frowned in thought. "Unless . . . ," she said, turning toward Jessica with a glint in her eyes.

"What?" Jessica asked, intrigued.

"Unless he's just *trying* to make you jealous," Lila said.

Jessica's heart dropped, but she started to smile. "No way."

"Think about it," Lila said, pulling off her expensive leather boots. "Jade's the first semiattractive female besides you that works there. He probably saw his opportunity and took it."

Jessica's posture straightened up a bit. "Ya think?" she asked.

"It's such a guy thing to do," Lila said.

Jessica laughed and brushed her hair back from her face. "Nothing like a good dose of Lila logic," she said.

Lila rolled her eyes. "Hey, I know it's been a while, but you might recall I'm hardly ever wrong."

"Whatever," Jessica said, smiling. The way she remembered it, Lila was almost never *right*—except in her own opinion.

But this *was* an interesting theory. *Trying* to make her jealous, huh? Well, two could play at that game. In fact, Jessica was very skilled at that game.

And Jeremy had no idea who he was dealing with.

*   *   *

Conner sauntered out into the parking lot and immediately spotted Elizabeth talking with Ken, Maria, and, of course, Tia.

Doesn't the girl have practice or something? he wondered irritably. He was beginning to feel like she was stalking him.

Conner's car was parked a few spaces down from Ken's. He'd have to walk right past them, and there was no way he was going to get away with that. Great. If his mood was bad when school started, it was particularly foul now. Socializing was definitely not on his after-school agenda.

Conner started walking at a fast clip, head down, eyes focused on his scuffed boots. Maybe he could slide past the group with a simple good-bye.

"Hey, Conner!" Ken called out.

Conner didn't even glance over. "Later." He could practically feel his Mustang pulling him over, but before he could get past his so-called friend, Elizabeth stepped away from them.

"Hey. Do you have a minute?" she asked.

Conner stopped and shoved his hands into his pockets. Just being close to her made his heart pound. *Yes*, he wanted to scream. *A minute, an hour. However long it takes to get through to you.*

But out of the corner of his eye he could see that Tia had her eyes glued on the two of them. Of course. The air was so crowded with uncomfortable vibes, he could almost choke. Maria was trying desperately not to stare, and Ken looked like he wanted to crawl out of his skin. Conner empathized.

He swallowed his frustration and tried to sound calm. "I've got a guitar lesson," he said loud enough for Tia to hear. Out of the corner of his eye he saw her shoulders relax.

That one small shift made Conner's blood boil. Since when did he run his life to please other people?

He reached out and took Elizabeth's hand, pulling her farther away so he could have a little privacy. This time he didn't even check to see if Tia was watching.

As soon as he was out of his friends' earshot, he stopped and turned to Elizabeth, never letting go of her hand. He was relieved to note that she didn't try to pull away.

"Can I call you later?" he asked Elizabeth quietly.

"I kind of wanted to talk to you in person," she said, her face close to his. "It's important."

Conner's heart jumped right up into his throat. Too important for the phone sounded bad. Way bad.

He studied her face. Strange. She didn't look upset at all. She actually looked kind of excited. His heartbeat slowed down slightly. She'd at least look angry or disgusted or something if she was going to dump him, right? Unless she was a fabulous actress and she wanted to torture him for another day first.

"Whatever you want," he managed to say, squeezing her palm slightly. "How about tomorrow after school?"

She nodded and graced him with a small smile. "Sounds good."

"Okay, then." Conner wanted more than anything to kiss her, but he wasn't sure how she'd take it. He just leaned forward and quickly brushed his lips against her cheek—fast enough to keep her from reacting and pushing him away. When he looked up, he saw Tia glance away, but he couldn't care less.

Because Elizabeth was still smiling.

TIA RAMIREZ

WAYS TO GET OVER THIS IDIOT CONNER THING

1. READ ALL MY OLD DIARY ENTRIES ABOUT HOW ANNOYING HE WAS IN MIDDLE SCHOOL

2. MAKE A LIST OF ALL THE GIRLS HE'S BEEN WITH AND DUMPED ALL OVER. (NOTE TO SELF: SET ASIDE A GOOD HOUR FOR THAT ONE. BRING IN ANDY AS CONSULTANT.)

3. LIST ALL THE THINGS THAT MADE ANGEL AN AMAZING BOYFRIEND. NOTE THAT CONNER DOES NOT SHARE ONE SINGLE QUALITY.

4. ~~PUT AWAY ALL PICTURES OF HIM.~~ NAH. TOO CHEESY.

5. ~~BURN ALL PICTURES OF HIM IN A RITUAL CLEANSING CEREMONY.~~ NAH. I THINK OUR FIRE EXTINGUISHER'S BUSTED.

6. TALK TO HIM. TELL HIM IT'S OVER . . . IF YOU CAN EVER GET HIM TO LOOK AT YOU AGAIN.

4

Jeremy stood behind the counter at House of Java on Wednesday evening, cleaning the steam wand on the huge espresso machine. Or at least he was pretending to clean it. Mostly he was watching Jade, who was across the room, refilling sugar dispensers.

He checked the pink fluorescent clock above the coffee thermoses. It was almost seven o'clock already. The after-dinner study crowd would be heading in any minute. It was now or never. He tried to push the jitters out of his stomach with a slow, deep breath.

"Get a grip, Aames," he told himself. "It's no big deal."

He made his shaking legs take him across the room, feeling like he'd just jumped off a high dive. No turning back now. The problem was he had no idea what he was going to say.

Fortunately, Jade gave him an opening. She was trying to unscrew the top of a sugar jar and having zero success.

Jeremy held out his hand and was gratified to

note that it wasn't shaking—visibly anyway. "Here, I'll get that."

"Thanks," Jade said with a smile.

When she handed him the jar, the tips of her fingers brushed across the back of his hand. Wow. Even that little touch sent a jolt through him.

Jeremy cleared his throat as the jar twisted open. "So, got any big plans for the weekend?" he asked, dumping what was left of the sugar into another jar she had already opened.

Jade glanced at him out of the corner of her eye. "I'm not sure yet. I always hate to commit to anything in case something better comes up."

"Oh, sure." Jeremy nodded. He wondered if his offer would be a "something better" or something she wouldn't care to commit to.

"How about you?" Jade asked, rearranging the sweetener packets in the cup in front of her.

"Depends." Now his hands *were* shaking as he screwed the top back on the sugar dispenser. He quickly set it down so she wouldn't see.

The bells on the front door tinkled, and two women in tennis outfits came in. Lovely. Now he had to get back to the counter.

Do it, the voice in his head screamed.

"I—I was wondering," he stammered, quickly wiping his palms on his jeans. Luckily Jade's back was turned to him as she continued straightening up. He wasn't sure he could handle asking her to her face. "Would you want to, you know, hang out on Friday night?"

Jade stopped wiping the self-service counter and turned slowly around. Relief flooded through Jeremy the moment he saw her face and its big, wide smile.

"Absolutely," she said with so much conviction, Jeremy nearly laughed.

Instead he swallowed hard. Inside, he was dancing across the room, but on the outside he made himself act calm, stuffing his hands in his front pockets and nodding slightly.

"Cool," he managed to say.

"What did you have in mind?" Jade asked.

"I hadn't actually thought that far." Jeremy immediately started to panic all over again. Jade wasn't exactly the pizza-and-miniature-golf kind of girl. He didn't want to suggest anything that would make him look like more of a geek than he already did. He shrugged. "Don't worry. I'll think of something."

Jade twisted a few strands of sleek, black hair around her finger and gave him a long, suggestive look. At least he was pretty sure it was meant to be suggestive. "I bet you will," she said.

Jeremy definitely wasn't prepared with an answer for *that*. "Great," he said. It was all he could come up with.

Luckily Jade smiled back. "Great."

*　　　*　　　*

Ken was so preoccupied driving home after practice, he almost drove right past his street. He'd rejoined the team weeks ago, and it still felt like garbage playing second-string behind Will Simmons. It felt almost as bad as not being on the team at all.

Almost.

He pulled his Trooper into the driveway, thankful that his dad's car wasn't there. Being around his father wasn't much fun lately, even when Ken was in a good mood. But after doing all the grunt work at practice, Ken was *sure* he couldn't handle talking to his dad. Not that his father had made much of an effort to speak to him anyway—not since he'd given up the starting-quarterback position.

As he unlocked the front door, Ken debated with himself over the real question of the hour. Nuke a Salisbury steak or a frozen enchilada dinner?

Both, he decided as he tossed his backpack on the living-room couch and headed for the kitchen. He was dragging. Running rollout after rollout so the offensive line could get themselves moving as one unit had tired him out. Two TV dinners might just give him enough energy to tackle his homework before he crashed.

Oddly, there was a grocery bag sitting on the counter by the fridge. Ken peeked inside. A bottle of champagne, a bunch of asparagus, and a couple of fishy-smelling packages wrapped in white butcher paper. The bottle still had frost on it. His father must have stopped at home and then run out again for something. Huh. Ken shoved the bag away from him. Looked like his dad was planning a romantic dinner.

Ken prayed it was with Asha.

He'd just ripped the enchilada dinner out of its box when he heard a rustling noise coming from the end of the hall near his father's room.

Ken froze. The dinner slid out of his hand and crashed to the floor. Someone was in the house. Ken quickly glanced around the room for a weapon but came up blank. Other than a couple of worn steak knives, there wasn't much around. He was just reaching for the champagne bottle when he heard a woman's voice.

"Ed?" the voice called out from down the hall. "You're home early."

Ken relaxed, but only slightly. The woman obviously knew his father, but it definitely wasn't Asha's voice. *What the hell?* He forgot about the bottle and walked out of the kitchen, peering down the hall.

"It's Ken," he called back. "My dad's not here."

Suddenly Faye, the woman who his dad was cheating on Asha with, walked out of his father's room with her hand on her hip. She narrowed her eyes at Ken for a split second and then sauntered toward him. She had long, skinny legs that looked even scrawnier since she was wearing high, pencil-thin heels. Her skirt and jacket were pressed and perfect, and her mousy brown hair was so blow-dried and lacquered with spray that Ken doubted it would move even in a cyclone.

The last time Ken had seen her, she'd been wet from the shower and wearing his father's bathrobe. Even then he'd found her unattractive, but all made up, she was like a horror show.

He wanted to glare at her, but he was too polite.

Faye stopped a few feet away from him and eyed him up and down. "Oh," she said. "It's you."

"Yeah," Ken said. "I mentioned that."

From the pinched look on her face, it was obvious she was less than happy to see him. But then again, she was kind of witchlike. Pinched might be her normal look, for all he knew.

"Ed told me there'd be nobody home," she said.

Ken couldn't think of anything polite to say, so he kept his mouth shut. He already felt like he'd crossed the propriety line with his sarcastic remark. Not that she'd even noticed it.

Faye produced a house key from her jacket pocket and dangled it in front of her. "Your father told me to make myself comfortable."

"That's nice." *Great,* Ken thought. *Now he's giving perfect strangers access to our house?*

"I'm making him dinner tonight," Faye continued. "You've eaten, haven't you? I wasn't planning on three." She looked him over again as if she was assessing exactly how much he could eat. "I definitely don't have enough food."

"Don't worry," Ken said as evenly as possible. "I can take care of myself. Just ignore me."

Like I'm planning to do to you, he added silently, turning toward the kitchen.

"I was counting on this to be a . . . special evening," Faye explained, giving him what he guessed was some kind of supermeaningful look. "We're having lobster and champagne. Having a teenager tromping around the house, playing loud music and whatever it is you do, is going to completely ruin the mood."

It was all Ken could do to keep from barfing at her feet. *Way too much information,* his brain screamed at him. He shuffled back a few steps. *Way, way too much information.*

"So what do you expect me to do?" Ken asked. This time he was unable to keep the disdain out of his voice.

"Your father works very hard, you know." She stared him down, hands back on hips. "He's entitled to a night off. Couldn't you run along and stay at a friend's house tonight?"

Ken's cheeks flamed with anger. Now she was ordering him out of his own house? He turned away, breaking eye contact, and for the first time noticed that the table in the formal dining room was set with candles and a big bouquet of flowers.

He was going to gag. No doubt about it now.

"So?" Faye said impatiently.

Ken was so mad, he literally couldn't talk. He thought he might just ram a fist through a wall. Not that he wanted to spend two more seconds with this witch, but the way she was basically drop kicking him out the door made him furious. And embarrassed that he didn't have the guts to tell her off. Even if she was a friend of his father's.

"It's a school night," he pointed out when he finally felt like he could speak. "I, um, have a lot of homework to do."

Faye gave him a nasty, Cruella de Vil kind of glare. "Well, can't you, *um*, do it at someone else's house?" she mocked him. Then she gave him a sickening smile. "Maybe we can all have a nice family dinner some other time."

Ken didn't trust himself to say a word. *Not if I can help it*, he thought.

He turned on his heel, tore through the living room, and grabbed his books and his jacket. He yanked the front door open so quickly, the knob slipped out of his hand and banged back against the wall. It made a pretty satisfying crash.

He was tempted to slam it for real on his way out, but he held back. The witch would probably tell his dad if he did that.

On second thought . . .

Ken reached out and slammed the door as hard as he possibly could.

*　　　*　　　*

Jeremy glanced at the clock for the fifth time in less than thirty seconds. He couldn't take it anymore. He had to go on his break. Ever since Jade had said yes, he'd been itching to grab some time alone and figure out what he was going to do with that yes. He had to come up with a good plan. Quick.

Ally pushed through the back-room door and walked out behind the counter. "Jeremy, you can—"

"Thanks!" Jeremy said, already untying his apron.

He shoved through the still swinging door and into the cluttered back room.

Jade said she'd go out with me. Jade. With me.

This had to be the best day ever. Jeremy wished he could yell. Or jump up and down. Or at least gloat to someone. But somehow he had a feeling that Ally and Corey, the only other two people working, wouldn't appreciate the story.

Jeremy headed straight for the magazine-covered coffee table. Since he knew he'd never be able to sit still on his break, he'd decided to snag a newspaper and do some research on possible cool date locales. He tossed aside a few horribly dated issues of *People* and grabbed a newspaper. Luckily it was that day's edition. Now all he had to do was find the Arts and Entertainment section, and he'd be good to go. But just as he was about to lower himself onto the beat-up maroon couch, the week's work schedule caught his eye.

Jeremy froze. He hadn't even thought to check if he was working on Friday.

He rushed over to the board and checked his name, then sighed with relief when he saw that he was off. But then he saw Jade's name, and his eyes widened.

Jade was, in fact, scheduled to work Friday.

Perfect.

Jeremy's shoulders slumped. Not only was she working on Friday, but he had shifts Saturday and Sunday night. There was no possible way they could go out this weekend.

Dropping the newspaper back onto the table, Jeremy headed back out front to tell Jade the bad news.

She was busing dishes at the last booth in the corner. "Hey, Jade?" Jeremy said. "About Friday night—"

Jade spun around to face him, her eyes bright. "Got a plan already?" she asked, resting the busing bucket on one hip. She looked him up and down. "You work fast. I like that."

He tried not to, he really did, but he felt himself blushing anyway. He ran a hand through his short brown hair.

"That's not it, actually," he said. "I just found out you're scheduled to work. Looks like we'll have to try again another time."

"Hey." Her dark eyes narrowed, and she put the bucket down on the table. "You're not canceling out on me, are you?"

"No. But I thought since you're—"

"Don't worry about work," she said, picking up a few saucers and placing them into the bucket with a clatter. "It's no problem. I'll think of something."

"Are you—," Jeremy started to ask, but snapped his mouth shut just in time. *If she says it's okay, it's okay.* She was probably just going to switch shifts with someone. Besides, she already thought he was a goody-goody, and her work schedule was her business, not his.

"Great," he said. "So we're still on?"

"I am if you are," she said, smiling as she gathered her things and walked past him. She touched his arm, sending another shot of shivers over his skin.

"Oh, I am," he said, grinning back. "I definitely, *definitely* am."

Senior Poll Category #7:
Most Talkative

Elizabeth Wakefield
Lila Fowler

Jessica Wakefield
Cherie Reese

Conner McDermott
Tia Ramirez

Ken Matthews
Lila Fowler, Amy Sutton

Will Simmons
Cherie Reese, Gina Cho

melissa Fox
Jessica Wakefield

Jade Wu
Amy Sutton

Maria Slater
There are just too many worthy candidates

TIA RAMIREZ
MELISSA FOX

Andy Marsden
Anyone who talks to me

Going My 5 Way?

Conner stepped out of the building after school on Thursday and blinked in the bright sunshine. The first thing he saw was Elizabeth, standing with a group of friends next to the flagpole. Luckily, for once no one Conner had ever spoken to was among the crowd.

Maybe something was finally going his way. Suddenly Elizabeth looked up and gave him a bright smile. Maybe a lot of things were finally going his way.

Conner jogged down the steps, the plaid shirt he wore open over his white tee flapping against his arms.

"Hey," Conner said when he reached Elizabeth's side.

"Hey," Elizabeth returned.

The little group eyed him with a mixture of curiosity and disdain. They were probably a bunch of *Oracle* writers, some of whom had heard through the grapevine that Conner was king of the pigs.

"Can we get out of here?" Conner reached for Elizabeth's hand before she could answer and pulled her away from the others.

"See you guys later!" Elizabeth called over her shoulder. She looked up at Conner, her forehead creased. "That was kind of rude."

"We're in a hurry," Conner said, heading for his car.

"We are?" Elizabeth asked, readjusting her book bag.

"Yup." He could hear the tinkling of her silver bracelets as he half dragged her along.

Finally Elizabeth laughed. "Okay, Conner, what's the big rush?" She pulled her hand out of his when they reached the Mustang and crossed her arms over her chest, but her eyes were amused.

"Today just sucked," Conner answered, walking around to the passenger-side door and unlocking it. "I can't wait to get out of here." He popped open the door and stepped back to let her in, but she didn't move. She just stared at him like he had nine heads.

"What?" Conner asked.

"Did you just open the car door for me?" she asked.

Conner looked down at his hand, which was still on the door handle. "Uh, yeah," he said.

Elizabeth walked up to him, the open door between them, and put her hand to his forehead. "You don't feel warm . . . ," she said with a smirk.

"Very funny," Conner said, feeling his cheeks start to burn.

Elizabeth laughed and lowered herself into the car, tucking her skirt under herself as she drew in her legs. Conner took a deep breath and closed the car door softly. In the two seconds it took him to walk around to the driver's side, he tried to calm his nerves.

He couldn't mess this up. No matter what happened. He couldn't lose Elizabeth.

"So let's go somewhere and talk," Conner said as he dropped into his seat and started the car.

"Sounds good to me," Elizabeth said.

She removed a loose barrette from her hair, and Conner watched her tuck the silky blond strands back into place and snap the barrette closed. As he pulled out of the space and into the street, he wondered if he'd ever touch her smooth hair again or feel it fall against his face while they were kissing.

Sure, Elizabeth seemed to be in good spirits, but that didn't mean he was in the clear. All his life Conner had found that even when he thought everything was fine, he was usually wrong.

An uncomfortable silence quickly filled the car, and Conner was grateful when Elizabeth switched on the radio to a local rock station.

Unfortunately, it wasn't enough to cure Conner's uneasiness. The car was stifling after baking in the sun all day, so Conner rolled down his window to let in some fresh air. Not that heat had much to do with the sweat prickling at his hairline and along his palms. Conner had been nervous about this moment for days, making it difficult to maintain the outer cool he was known for. He propped his elbow on the window frame and tried to look like all that was on his mind was enjoying a drive on a gorgeous day with his girlfriend.

But *was* she still his girlfriend? Did he still *want* a girlfriend? And if he did, what had he been thinking when he'd kissed Tia? Twice?

Conner tried not to hold the wheel in a death grip. Wasn't this just typical of his completely screwed-up life? He dreaded what Elizabeth was going to say to him when he had no clue what he wanted himself.

Except a drink. Even a sip. Anything to calm his nerves. Once he knew what was going on with Elizabeth, one way or the other, he wouldn't need the alcohol anymore. He was sure of it. But right now, it sounded like a great solution.

He threaded his way through the after-school traffic until he hit Ocean Way. The traffic there was a lot lighter, and he didn't have to pay such strict attention to the road. He stole a glance at Elizabeth. She was scrunched low in her seat, her head laid back against the upholstery. Her eyes were closed. Conner wondered if she was just re-laxing or if she was pretending to relax so she wouldn't have to break up with him while he was driving.

Once they hit Highway 1, he turned north for no particular reason. He wanted to get this over with, but it was almost like part of him just wanted to keep on driving forever. No worries. No demands.

No gut-wrenching pain in the near future.

Without giving it much thought, Conner took the last turnoff for Crescent Beach. Beautiful, remote, romantic Crescent Beach. Make-out spot for the entire teenage population of Sweet Valley. The ones with cars anyway.

He glanced at her out of the corner of his eye as he followed the road down to the parking lot above the beach. He couldn't see her expression because she was looking out the window at the water.

The sun was in front of her, and the ocean breeze was gently blowing strands of her golden hair back from her face. In that instant, with the sun and the crisp, clean salt air all around her, Conner thought that she might just be the only thing in his life that wasn't broken or needy or screwed up beyond belief.

If he could just hold on to her.

There wasn't another car in sight. He picked a place where they could watch the waves and parked. The instant the engine died, the car was filled with the rhythmic crash of breaking waves and the cawing of shorebirds picking at the wet sand. Any other time, Conner supposed the sounds would be soothing. Today all he could think about was that he'd probably managed to flush one of the better things in his life right down the toilet.

He laced his fingers together on top of the steering wheel and stared out at the long line of a building wave. "So," he forced himself to say. "What did you want to talk about?"

For the first time since Jeremy had started working at House of Java, he found himself barreling through the door fifteen minutes late for his shift. Late. He couldn't believe it. And he didn't even have a good excuse. He'd just spent too much time messing around with the guys after football practice.

Something was definitely wrong with him.

"I'm so sorry, Jess," he said as he rushed behind the counter and punched in. He tossed his stuff in the back room and grabbed an apron, tying it on so fast, he did it inside out. "What can I do?" he asked, practically panting as he slid into place next to her.

"Don't worry," Jessica said with a quick laugh. "I'll get this one." She looked up at the young mother waiting at the counter. The woman had three little redheaded kids climbing all over her and looked more than a little frazzled. "A double half-caf espresso and three children's hot chocolates," Jessica repeated the order.

"That's it," the woman said, fishing in her pocket-book for her wallet and coming up with a rattle.

Jessica leaned into Jeremy's side as she reached past him for a cappuccino mug. Leaned a little too far and a little too long. Weird. Finally Jeremy moved away to give her some space.

She smiled up at him and tucked a strand of hair back behind her ear. "Oops." She giggled and bit her lower lip in her classic shy-but-with-something-behind-it way. "'Scuze me."

Jeremy shuffled backward farther until his butt hit the edge of the counter.

She's not flirting with you, Aames, he thought. *Get over yourself.*

Then Jessica smiled flirtatiously at him and pushed the button on the machine to pull a double espresso. Jeremy turned away and took a second to redo his apron. Okay, so she was acting a little more . . . *friendly* than usual, but that wasn't really a big deal, right?

Besides, maybe his mad rush to get here had just affected his brain.

"So, what happened to you?" Jessica asked when she'd given her customer her change. "Did football practice run over?"

See? A perfectly normal question.

"Nah," Jeremy said, leaning back against the counter. "I was more smelly than usual, so I took an extra-long shower," he joked.

"Well, it didn't work," Jessica said, scrunching up her nose.

Jeremy smiled. They were bantering like they always did. He felt like an idiot for thinking she might be interested again. Jessica had made her feelings very clear on numerous occasions.

"Speaking of smells . . ." Jessica stretched her arm out under his nose. "I got this perfume at Sedona last week," she said. "Liz says it's too sweet for me. What do you think?"

Jeremy took a quick glance at her face. She was looking at him expectantly. *Oookay,* he thought sarcastically. He pushed off from the counter and maneuvered around her.

"It's, uh, fine," he mumbled. A middle-aged guy with a newspaper stuffed under his arm was just walking up to the counter. "Can I help you?" Jeremy asked quickly.

"Yeah, I'd like a latte," the man said.

"That's two-fifty," Jeremy said, hitting the button and trying to ignore the odd look Jessica was giving him. He took the man's money and tossed it into the drawer. "I'll bring your drink out to you," he said.

"You don't have to—"

"That's okay," Jeremy told him. "I have to bus the tables anyway."

He hurried to deliver the drink before Jessica could ask him what his problem was. Warm milk foam sloshed across the back of his hand as he walked, but he barely noticed. Ever since Jeremy had started paying attention to Jade, Jessica had been acting weird—either biting people's heads off or being way too nice. At this point all he wanted was to stay as far away from her as he could for the rest of the shift.

That should be easy to do behind a box-sized counter.

Jeremy gave his customer the latte and then took his time busing tables. He stole a glance at Jessica while he picked up napkins and wiped coffee rings off the end table next to the old flowered couch.

Sure enough, she was staring at him over the top of the cash register. Jeremy felt himself start to blush and quickly averted his eyes. What the heck was he supposed to do? If Jessica *did* like him—

Suddenly Jessica laughed, and Jeremy looked up again.

She was standing behind the counter with Danny, and she was giving him that same flirty smile she'd been turning on Jeremy lately. Then she laughed at something Danny said, put a hand square in the middle of his chest, and gave him a playful shove.

That was definitely flirting. Jeremy scrubbed at a stubborn spot on the wood. He wasn't exactly an expert, but laughing and touching seemed like they pretty much covered it.

So maybe it wasn't just him. Maybe Jessica was

just a flirt in general. Maybe he'd just never noticed before.

He'd definitely never noticed that it bugged him before.

He hated to admit it, but part of him even felt sort of jealous. Which was completely crazy because another part of him wanted Jessica to move on, to leave him free to date Jade.

Jeremy almost groaned out loud. When did everything get so complicated?

He worked his way to the self-serve table, where the cream and sugar were kept, so he could be close enough to hear what Jessica and Danny were saying. He picked up the syrup dispenser full of honey and slowly wiped the sticky drips from the outside while he listened in.

Jessica jumped up and snatched Danny's cap off his head. "Ha. Got it."

Danny laughed and made a grab for his hat. "Hey—give it back."

"Make me." Jessica held the cap behind her back, making Danny feint right and left around her. She kept giggling and letting out the occasional squeal. Finally Danny grabbed her by the waist and started tickling her.

Okay, Jeremy decided, she was *definitely* flirting. And he had definitely moved on. And he was okay with it. Sort of.

*   *   *

Tell me I'm not toast, Conner prayed.

He was too nervous to look at Elizabeth. He just watched the waves rise up and then slam down on themselves, morphing from a glassy green tube into a froth of white foam while he waited for her to talk.

"I want to talk about us," Elizabeth said, answering his earlier question.

No surprises there.

"Okay," Conner said cautiously. He forced his fingers to relax around the steering wheel.

She turned to face him. "I think we have some things to straighten out."

You have no idea, he thought, unable to meet her gaze.

She fiddled with her bracelets, sliding them up and down her slender arm. "I think I overreacted about that whole thing between you and Tia," she said softly. "I was so mad and so hurt at first, I—"

"You had a right to be," Conner said, hating how hoarse his voice sounded.

"Well, I don't know what Tia told you, but I kind of freaked out on her the other day," Elizabeth said, averting her gaze.

"You did?"

"I can't believe she didn't tell you." Elizabeth picked at her nails like there was no tomorrow.

She was probably too busy kissing me, Conner thought, tightening his grip on the steering wheel again.

"Well, I guess it doesn't matter, then," Elizabeth said. She took a deep breath and looked at him for the first time. "There's something I have to tell you," she said slowly.

There was a long, silent pause. A pause that made Conner so sick to his stomach, he thought he was going to die right there. Then she suddenly reached up, touched her soft palm to his cheek, leaned forward, and kissed him quickly. The relief he felt was beyond compare. Then she pulled away, pressed her forehead to his, and whispered so quietly he could barely hear her.

"I love you, Conner."

The chill that went through him seemed to push the words up out of his mouth. "I love you too."

She smiled, and Conner had never seen anything so perfect in his life. He touched her face and kissed her and realized he'd never felt so completely happy before.

Even though he'd just said the words he'd promised himself he'd never hear himself say.

When they parted, Conner simply felt stunned. For the past few days he'd practically convinced himself he didn't even want a girlfriend, but now everything was different. Elizabeth loved him. She was so good and pure and perfect, and she loved him. What had he done to deserve this?

Nothing, a little voice inside him answered. *You've done everything to prove you don't deserve this.*

"Conner?" he heard her say, forcing him to snap back to reality. Something about her tone made him feel like she'd just read his mind. "There's just one thing," she said.

He pulled back until he could see her face but took her hand in his. He suddenly didn't want to stop touching her. Ever. "What?"

"Don't get mad, okay?"

Conner swallowed hard. "Okay."

"I'm trying to be . . . you know . . . *mature* about this—I really am. And I want us all to stay friends." She stared down at their hands. "I talked to Tia and everything, and she said you don't . . ." She paused, taking a deep breath. "I just need to hear you say it," she continued, looking up at him. "Tell me you're not interested in her in . . . that way."

Conner knew what the answer was, even if all his actions of the past few days proved otherwise.

"I'm not," he said firmly, looking her directly in the eye. With gentle fingers he smoothed a strand of hair off her face. "I am *not* interested in Tia."

Elizabeth laughed shakily in obvious relief and squeezed his hand. "That's definitely good to know."

Conner pulled her to him and held her close, feeling himself lighten as she squeezed back. Suddenly everything was perfect.

But for how long?

The reasonable part of his brain made him admit

he actually had no clue what he wanted from one minute to the next.

Still, he knew what he needed.

He needed Elizabeth.

She made his world sane.

Conner eased his arms from around her shoulders and tilted her face gently up until their eyes met. "I haven't been interested in anybody else since the day I met you," he said. Which, he reassured himself, was strictly true.

Elizabeth's lips spread into a slow, satisfied smile. "Conner McDermott, did you just say something romantic?"

"Don't get used to it," Conner said with a grin.

She laughed again, and Conner lowered his mouth to hers and kissed her—really kissed her—for the first time in way too long.

He'd done it. He'd gotten her back. And they were in love.

Now everything else in his screwed-up life would fall into place too.

And this time I won't let it blow up in my face, he swore to himself. *This time things are going to change.*

Elizabeth Wakefield

Sometimes I wish I had Jessica's life. Well, okay, not her <u>entire</u> life. I don't want her grades. And she can keep the cheerleading. But I kind of envy her relationships. They're so simple.

Unlike my completely bizarre soap opera of a life.

It's not like I'm the most secure person on the planet to begin with. And I've always known Tia and Conner share something special that I'm not part of. I know he shares more of his feelings with her.

And even though he said he loves me, and we're back together, and I know Conner wants to be with me, I can't help worrying a little.

After all, this has been a total disaster. I mean, finding your boyfriend in bed with your friend is something straight out of <u>One Life to Live.</u>

And they're both so hard to read. I mean, I've always thought Tia was an honest person, but I know she's hiding something. I can feel it. And Conner. Well, who knows what really goes on behind that intent brooding look of his? I'm getting better at understanding him, but I'm not all the way there yet. You'd think once the words are said—<u>I love you</u>— everything would fall into place. But it doesn't. It actually gets even messier.

A lot messier. There's more at stake now, you know?

But with Jess things are so clear-cut. They always have been. She and her girlfriends have always had a strict policy when it comes to guys.

All bets are off. Every woman for herself. Winner takes all.

Sounds sick, right?

Well, at least it's up front.

CHAPTER
I Don't Think So
6

Ken trotted up to the front door of his house on Thursday evening, still smiling over the intense good-night kiss he and Maria had just shared. Even though last night had sucked, today he'd pretty much decided life was good. He'd had a great dinner at Maria's house, an even better kiss, and only one lame paragraph to write for English tonight.

The phone started to ring just as he got his key in the lock, but he didn't hurry, figuring his dad would answer it. Then he remembered that his father was out on a date with Asha tonight.

Thank God. Hopefully the guy would wake up soon and realize that Asha was fifty times cooler and fifty times cuter than that Faye witch. Then life really would be good. If only.

Ken twisted his key in the lock and shoved the door open on the third ring. He hurdled the coffee table in the living room and sprinted for the kitchen, but before he could grab the phone, the answering machine picked up.

Oh, well. Ken decided to take the extra second to

catch his breath. He could always pick up after whoever it was started talking. Besides, he hated taking long, complicated messages from the sports desk at the newspaper. If it was them, they'd be better off recording a message.

Ken waited by the kitchen counter, tapping a pencil on the pad of paper his father kept next to the wall phone. Finally the taped greeting finished and the caller started speaking. The female voice immediately set Ken's teeth on edge.

It was, of course, Faye.

"Hi, Ed." Her throaty voice invaded his kitchen. "Faye here. Thanks again for the other night. I had a wonderful time." She drew out each word like some actress playing the evil other woman in a cheesy TV movie. It was like she knew the role she was filling.

Ken rolled his eyes. *Gag me,* he thought.

"Anyway, I was thinking," she continued. "The buyers from Chicago canceled on me, so I've got tomorrow night free. How about you?"

Ken started sketching a dagger on the message pad, but he pressed down too hard, and the pencil tip broke off.

"Give me a call. I'll see you soon." She finished speaking, and the sound of the dial tone blared through the speaker for a moment before quickly cutting off.

Ken threw down the pencil, and it bounced all the way across the kitchen, landing in the sink with a clatter. He glared at the blinking message light for a long time.

I could just erase it, he thought, his finger poised over the erase button. Then his father wouldn't get the message and he wouldn't call her back. And Faye seemed like exactly the kind of person who wouldn't tolerate one little oversight like that. End of relationship. End of problem.

Except Ken had no right to interfere in his father's life. He knew that. Even if his father was hurting Asha and making an idiot out of himself. That was his decision. Ken lowered his hand and closed his eyes.

It's just one little message, he thought. *It could just as easily get eaten by the machine.*

And suddenly he was staring at the blinking light again. His dad had been acting like a complete moron lately. It was obvious the man didn't know what he was doing. Wasn't that cause for a major exception? Ken crossed his arms over his chest. Would it really be wrong to protect his father from himself when he was temporarily insane?

No, it wouldn't.

Before he could change his mind, Ken pushed the erase button. Faye's message played through at high speed as the machine deleted it.

"I'll see you soon!" she chirped like a chipmunk on helium.

Ken smiled grimly. "I don't think so, Faye."

*   *   *

"Found it!" Andy yelled, slapping his desk in triumph. Then he looked around his empty room sheepishly.

With a click of the mouse he was logged on to a Web site for gay teens. For a whole minute he simply stared at the computer screen. From this site he could jump to pages with advice on coming out, dating, religion and homosexuality. He could even join discussion groups for gay kids his age.

Stupid, but he almost felt like he was going to cry. It was like finding a whole different world. One he might actually belong in. And that was partly why he was here. To find out for sure if he really did belong.

He clicked on the message board and scrolled through the postings. Reading messages from guys across the country, it hit him for the first time that he wasn't the only person in the world who was utterly confused. All the second-guessing, the wanting to like girls and be "normal," were things the other guys struggled with too.

```
If you're having these feelings,
you just have to accept them. It
actually helped me to tell some of my
best friends. I know it's different
for everyone, but the more I said it
out loud, the more comfortable I was
with it.
```

Andy sighed and stared at the message. He'd been trying to talk about it with his friends, but so far he'd had no luck.

But he sort of felt like he was ready to tell someone. That he was ready to say out loud that he was gay. Ever since he'd realized he had feelings for Travis Hanson, Andy had been telling himself maybe. Possibly. It was in the realm of reality. But the more his friends pushed him aside, the more Andy was forced to look at himself and see the truth.

It was real. And he really wanted to deal with it.

He clicked through some more messages, searching for further advice about talking to friends. But suddenly the instant-message box filled his screen.

```
lizw:    You're busted, mister.
```

Andy jerked his hands away from the keyboard. Wait. There was no way she could tell what site he was logged on to, was there?

```
lizw:    Caught you fooling around on
         the Web. Try to tell me
         you're doing research for a
         class. Just try it.
```

Andy laughed nervously. She was just messing with him. But when he typed back, his fingers were shaking.

```
marsden1:Ha ha.
lizw:    Thought so :) You got a
         minute?
marsden1:I'm sort of in the middle of
         something here.
lizw:    It's about Conner. And Tia.
marsden1:Surprise, surprise.
              <DELETE>
```

He sighed and banged away at the keys.

```
marsden1:Shoot.
lizw:    I decided to give him another
         chance, and I'm glad I did,
         but I'm so freaked out. Do you
         think I did the right thing? I
         mean, is he going to dump me
         for Tia or something? Heeeelp!
```

Andy stared at the blinking cursor. He didn't want Elizabeth to get hurt, but he couldn't betray Tia's confidence either.

He felt his blood start to boil. Why did Tia and Conner have to tell him everything in the first place? The last thing he needed right now was to be caught in the middle of a love triangle.

```
lizw:    Andy, are you there?
marsden1:Yes, unfortunately
              <DELETE>
```

```
marsden1:Right here. I wish I could
         help, but I'm not exactly the
         person to ask about
         relationships right now.
         Trust me.
lizw:    Am I really talking to Andy?
         Andy of the witty one-
         liners? Andy of the sage advice?
marsden1:It's me.
lizw:    So, c'mon! Do I trust them or
         what? What do I do?
```

Andy groaned and tapped his head lightly against the monitor. He wondered if he could just log off and pretend his connection had gotten fried. He held the cursor over the log-off button, but then his conscience got the better of him and he moved it away.

Besides, she'd probably just call on the phone if he didn't get this over with now.

```
marsden1:Okay. Let's take what we
         know. You know Tia wouldn't
         hurt you on purpose, right?
lizw:    Agreed.
marsden1:And let's even say they both
         went temporarily psycho.
lizw:    Not hard to believe that :)
marsden1: I don't know why it happened,
         but I think they both feel bad.
```

```
                I'm sure Tia does. And they're
                not going to get together.
                Conner only wants to be with
                you. That I know for sure.
lizw:           Really?
marsden1:Really.
lizw:           Thanks, Andy. I actually do feel
                better. What's new with you?
```

Andy hesitated, his fingers frozen above the keyboard. Amazing how a simple question could make him want to spill his guts. He was getting so damn tired of holding this all inside. He felt like he could type three pages without stopping.

Maybe he should.

This was Elizabeth, after all. Calm, thoughtful Elizabeth. If he had a friend levelheaded enough to help him sort through this, she was the one.

```
marsden1: Do you think it's weird I spend
          more time watching Buffy's
          vampire boyfriend than Buffy?
lizw:     Not at all. So you're not a
          Sarah Michelle Gellar fan. So
          what? Conner can't stand her.
marsden1: No, that's not what I mean. I
          mean
```

He hesitated. Elizabeth had a lot going on right now herself. Was it really fair to dump all this on her?

Andy sighed. Probably not. Even rock-solid, down-to-earth Elizabeth had space in her head only for her own problems at the moment. He hit the delete key.

```
marsden1:Okay, so that's good I'm not
         weird. Just checking. You
         have to stay on top of these
         sorts of things, right?
lizw:    Absolutely. You are one
         hundred percent not weird.
         Feel better?
marsden1:Oh, yeah.
```

Jessica smiled brightly at the incredibly cute college guy standing across the counter from her at House of Java. His sideburns were a little too long and his hair a little too unkempt, but he was hot enough for her purposes.

"Where did you get that?" she asked, eyeing his well-worn brown leather bomber jacket. "It's so cool."

His gray eyes flicked over her from head to toe, and he gave her an appreciative grin. "Thanks. It was a gift."

Jessica slid the cardboard cup across the counter toward him, making sure she held on to it until his fingers brushed hers.

"Here you go," she said in a deeper-than-necessary voice. "One espresso macchiato with hazelnut syrup to go."

"Thanks." He nodded, giving her one last, warm look. "Later," he said quietly.

"Definitely." Jessica made sure she turned a bit to the right so he would catch her smile from its best angle. She wasn't proud of it, but she used to spend hours in front of the mirror, testing different expressions on herself. She hadn't done it in a while, but at the moment she was glad she had once been that shallow.

And the guy seemed to appreciate it too. She was sure she saw him blush as he walked away. Jessica just hoped none of this little exchange was lost on Jeremy, who was busy refilling the Sweet'n Low packets at the self-serve counter.

She smoothed the emerald green apron down over her hips and stole a glance at her ex, just in time to see him glance away. *Ha!* She'd caught him red-handed, and she wanted to laugh out loud.

Excellent. Let's see how he likes it.

They had only an hour more until closing, and she'd managed to flirt with at least a dozen guys right under his nose. And he was noticing. She could tell that she was getting to him by the droop of his shoulders as he carried the tray of dishes back to the kitchen.

Oh, well.

He should have thought of that before he decided to flirt with Jade just to make her jealous. The next time she saw Lila, she was going to have to kiss the girl for pointing out the obvious.

Jessica looked around the half-empty café. No customers were waiting for drinks at the moment, so she took a second to lean her forearms on the counter and take some weight off her aching feet. She was really going to have to remind herself that cork-soled sandals were not the way to go for a four-hour shift.

Jessica glanced over at the cappuccino machine and thought about making herself a quick short half caf but then decided against it. She was pretty sure that if she ingested any more caffeine, her veins were going to burst from pumping too hard.

Jeremy rounded the counter and slid past her, taking care not to let any part of his body touch hers, even though he was carrying a tray full of dirty mugs and plates. A smirk twisted its way onto Jessica's face when she heard the dishes clanking in the kitchen behind her. Jeremy must be loading the big commercial dishwasher—with a little extra vigor. He didn't normally make that much noise back there.

Could it be because he was angry? Jealous, even?

Jessica allowed herself a little laugh. It was almost too easy. Maybe next time he would be a tad less obvious about his game playing.

"I mean, *Jade?*" Jessica muttered to herself. What could Mr. Citizenship Award, Mr. Perfect Attendance, have in common with a sarcastic, flirtatious party girl like Jade Wu?

Jessica wiggled her toes. She had to hand it to him, though. It wasn't a bad plan.

She would have done the same thing in his position. Unfortunately for him, he'd messed with the wrong girl. Jessica could outflirt Jeremy any day of the week.

The door to the back room suddenly swung open, and Jessica straightened up. Jeremy walked out and went immediately to the sink to wash his hands. Jessica scanned the room and noticed that the two semicute guys who'd come in an hour earlier were still hanging out in the cushy red velvet booth near the corner. And it looked like they'd finished their Italian sodas.

Perfect. There might just be time to hit Jeremy between the eyes one more time before closing.

Jessica stepped out from behind the counter and walked slowly toward the guys' table, head high. It took her about two seconds to make eye contact with cute boy number one. She could feel Jeremy watching her.

She stopped in front of the table and smiled.

"Hey, guys," she said, putting her hands on their shoulders. "Anything else I can get you?"

"How about a date?" the shorter one asked.

Jessica laughed and with one practiced shake of her head flipped her hair back over her shoulder. "I was thinking about something from the menu, actually, but thanks."

While the two guys debated over having a couple more sodas, Jessica very casually glanced around behind her as if she were simply checking out the store. Jeremy was standing behind the counter, restocking the tea bags and trying very hard not to look at her.

Jessica quickly turned back to her customers, but now her grin was totally genuine.

This is good, she thought. *This is all very good.*

Maria Slater

Today in world literature we started reading <u>Anna Karenina,</u> and I read a line that really hit me. "All happy families resemble one another. Every unhappy family is unhappy in its own way." So Tolstoy is saying that dysfunctional families make interesting literature, I guess. Okay, I'll agree with him on that one.

It's not so interesting <u>living</u> in an unhappy family, though. I should know. Things are a lot better since Mom and Dad started realizing how much more attention they pay to Nina and how they've expected me to live up to her standards.

Did I say live up to? More like turn into her.

And my parents aren't the only ones. They might be the most obvious about it, but they're definitely not alone.

Why can't parents just accept us for who we are instead of trying to turn us into the people they need us to be?

CHAPTER 7
Serious Fun

Conner drove home after school on Friday, feeling restless. He had tons of homework to catch up on, but he didn't think he could make himself sit still. Unfortunately, Elizabeth was working at Sedona until closing, and he definitely didn't want to see Tia.

He swung by the Burger Barn drive through and picked up a large soda, enjoying the light, heady feeling that came from having no obligations for the moment. It would have been nice to see Elizabeth. Ever since their conversation at the beach yesterday, Conner hadn't been able to get her out of his mind—not that he wanted to. He just kept hearing her say those words over and over again.

"I love you, Conner." Sometimes he felt like he'd dreamed it. He *knew* he didn't deserve it. And he also knew that he was going to find a way to mess it up and lose it, so he wanted to spend as much time with her as he could before she woke up and realized what a waste he was.

But there would be no QT with Elizabeth tonight

unless Conner felt like getting a makeover at the mall. Not in this lifetime.

Maybe Evan was free. They could go to the Riot or, if nothing was happening there, maybe head up to Crescent Beach and see if any of the old El Carro crowd was hanging out.

A bonfire and a beer would really hit the spot.

He sucked down the soda as he drove toward his friend's house. When he turned the corner onto Akers Avenue, Andy's huge vintage Cadillac stuck out like a billboard in his driveway across the street from Evan's house.

A twinge of guilt started to seep its way into Conner's chest. He hadn't spent much time with Andy lately, and the guy had been looking almost as stressed out as *Conner* felt. On impulse he parked next to Andy's house and headed across the lawn.

Ignoring the front door, Conner scooped up a handful of gravel from the walkway and chucked it gently at Andy's bedroom window.

"Hey, Marsden, you computer geek," he yelled. "Where you hiding?"

Andy's dog, Casey, woofed loudly. A second later the window opened and Andy's curly red hair popped into view. Sure enough, behind him Conner saw the whitish glow of his computer monitor.

"Hey!" Andy yelled, obviously angry. He paused when he caught a glimpse of Conner. "Oh, it's you. I guess the front door's too normal for you these days, huh?"

Conner grinned. "Damn straight."

Andy frowned and muttered something that sounded oddly like, "I wish." Conner had no idea what that could mean, so he chose to ignore it.

"So you gonna spend Friday night with your computer or what?" Conner asked, stuffing his hands in the pockets of his beat-up suede jacket.

Casey put his huge paws up on the windowsill next to Andy and barked happily at Conner. His head was almost on the same level as his owner's. Andy scratched him behind the ears. "Depends on the options, my man."

"I'm going to go drag Evan out of his house in about two seconds," Conner said. "Let's go over to the Riot, see what's happening."

"I don't know," Andy answered, shaking his head. "I don't really think I have the energy for that. I was kind of counting on making a big dent in the couch with my butt."

Conner smirked. "High aspirations," he said.

"Hey!" Andy exclaimed, his eyes brightening. "My parents are going to a dinner party after work. They won't be home until late. Why don't you guys come over here? We could order pizza and hang out by the pool."

"I'm too wound up," Conner said, absently punching his right hand into his left. Sitting around and talking was the last thing he wanted to do. That would mean having to explain about the whole Tia thing and how he was handling it. There was no way he wanted to go there tonight. Not even with his good friends.

"Come on," Andy prodded, leaning his arms on the windowsill. "I could use some advice, actually."

Conner kicked at the gravel surrounding the bushes below Andy's window and shrugged. "We can talk at the Riot."

"It's not that kind of talking," Andy said gravely— a tone Conner had never heard from Andy before.

Conner studied his friend's pale, drawn face. Except for the freckles sprinkled across his nose, Andy looked like he was turning into a vampire. This guy needed a party worse than Conner did.

"As your friend, it's my duty to point out that you're not exactly living up to your legendary party-animal status lately, Andrew," Conner said.

"No kidding." Andy smiled tiredly. "I'm thinking about retiring my crown."

"Not allowed," Conner replied. Andy averted his eyes and stared out across the lawn. Conner had the distinct feeling that he was supposed to ask what was wrong, but the whole idea made him uncomfortable. He'd never been good at talking about feelings—his or anyone else's. "You're not planning to take down the school-district computer system or something, are you?" Conner asked finally.

Andy snorted, seeming to come back down to earth for a moment. "Like *that* would be any kind of challenge." His smile dissolved quickly, and he went somber again.

Conner was starting to run out of patience. "C'mon, man," he insisted, backing up slightly. He was more than ready to get out of here, whether Andy was coming with him or not. "It's Friday night, and you're a single guy now. You should be out on the prowl."

Andy gave him a tight smile. "Thanks, but I really can't. You crazy kids will just have to take on Sweet Valley on your own."

Conner shrugged and continued to back up. "You sure?"

Andy nodded, but he wasn't even facing Conner anymore. "I'm sure."

Before Conner had even turned around, Andy had shut his window and clicked the lock. Conner practically jogged over to Evan's. Andy's sober thing had started to bring him down, and he just didn't have time for that now. For once in his life, Conner was ready to have some serious fun. And he wasn't going to let the opportunity pass him by.

Jessica rolled her eyes and sighed loudly into the phone. Yet another answering machine telling her to speak at the beep. As soon as the tone sounded, she rushed through her speech.

"Hi, this message is for Danny. Danny, it's Jessica from House of Java. I was wondering if you could possibly work tonight. This place is insane, and it would really help me out. So, um, please call me back when you get in if you can. Thanks."

She slammed the handset back into the cradle of the stupid Princess phone on Ally's desk.

Great. Just great.

After four answering machines, three parents, and a little sister, she'd had absolutely no luck getting a replacement for Jade tonight. Why wasn't anybody home on a Friday afternoon?

Jade had better be puking her guts out, Jessica decided. Nothing less was going to get her off the hook for calling in sick all of ten minutes before her shift started.

Everyone had been complaining to Ally that they were short staffed on Friday nights as it was. And now, with Ally out of town and one less person working, Jessica had a feeling she was in for a nightmare. Maybe being promoted to assistant manager wasn't going to be such a great thing after all.

Jessica leaned back in Ally's rickety chair and let out a long, slow breath, studying the work schedule pinned up above the desk. She'd already tried every single employee except Jeremy, but tonight was his first night off in almost two weeks. There was no way she could do that to him.

Then she imagined the endless stream of customers

100

she was about to be bombarded with and reached for the phone anyway.

She dialed two numbers and then slammed the phone down again. No way. Jeremy had worked a zillion hours already, and he was scheduled for the next night too. If anybody deserved a night off, it was him.

Jessica was just going to have to figure this out.

Or sacrifice her sanity trying.

Jeremy walked a step behind Jade as they headed down Main Street toward the restaurant he had chosen for their date. He'd already started wondering if he should have paid more attention to his clothes. Jade looked so cool, and he looked like a prep-school reject.

He pressed a hand down over his blue oxford shirt. Maybe he should have gone for something more daring than a button-down and khakis. As if he had anything more daring in his closet.

Jade, of course, was dressed to kill. Her entire outfit was black—a tight mini that showed off her slim hips and legs and a fitted black top that ended just above her belly button. Over that she wore a vintage black sweater with little beads sewn into the front. For a purse she had an old black leather camera case strung across her chest. He loved the way she'd tied her silky black hair back with a slender ribbon and rimmed her exotic-looking eyes with dark makeup.

"Here it is," Jeremy said, breaking the silence when they reached the restaurant.

He held open the door for her and breathed a huge sigh of relief as she grinned up at him. At least Trent had been right about the restaurant. Tutto Mare, the newest place on Main Street, *was* beyond hip. The walls were old brick, except the very back wall, which was floor-to-ceiling glass overlooking a lighted patio. All the ceiling lamps and even the tables and chairs were a spare, Art Deco sort of style. The place reminded Jeremy of some ultracool restaurant set on *Friends* or something.

"Wow," Jade said as they stepped inside. She nodded discreetly toward the twenty-something professionals sitting at the bar. "Check out those outfits."

Jeremy squeezed in the door behind her. "Yeah," he said lamely. The men at the bar looked like they'd just walked out of *GQ* magazine. Jeremy was about ready to give up and go home.

Chill out, man, he told himself. *Since when do you care about your clothes?*

"Excuse me." A waiter in black pants and a white, Oriental-looking jacket squeezed in between Jeremy and Jade and headed to the back of the restaurant.

Jade moved closer to Jeremy until their shoulders were touching. She sniffed the air and took his hand, causing a fierce blush to take over his face.

"It smells wonderful in here," Jade said.

"Sure does," he replied, commenting more on her

perfume than the smell of the food. He held her hand gently, enjoying the way her smaller fingers fit in his.

He was going to have to remember to thank Trent tomorrow. The cool restaurant might even make up for his lame fashion sense.

The maitre d' greeted them with two menus the size of skateboards in his hands. "By the fireplace or out on the deck?" he asked.

Jeremy turned to Jade. "What do you think?"

Jade squeezed his hand and pulled him toward her until their bodies were touching from shoulder to hip. "Definitely the fireplace. It's more romantic," she said softly.

A jolt of electricity zinged from the top of Jeremy's head right down through his feet. He cleared his throat.

"The fireplace it is," he said, amazed to find that his voice didn't crack from nervousness.

As soon as they were seated, the waiter hurried over to take their drink orders.

"Might I suggest an appetizer?" he asked. "The New Zealand oysters are exceptional tonight. We just got them in today."

Jeremy wondered exactly how many paychecks a serving of seafood flown halfway around the world would run, but he pushed the thought away. It had been a long time since he'd been out on a date. He wasn't going to think about the money.

"Oooh, oysters," Jade said, her dark eyes sparkling. "Yeah, let's."

"Sounds good to me," Jeremy said, causing the waiter to scurry off toward the kitchen. Jeremy leaned into the table as soon as the guy was out of earshot. "I've never had oysters," he confessed.

"You're kidding!" Jade said with an edge of sarcasm. "You do live in California, don't you?"

Jeremy felt his face heat up again, but luckily the waiter was back quickly with a plate of slimy-looking things in mottled gray shells. *Yuck* was the first word that came to Jeremy's mind. He leaned forward, but they didn't look any better up close.

"They're raw," he pointed out.

Jade laughed. "They're an aphrodisiac."

"Seriously?" Jeremy wrinkled his nose. "They look like snot." Then he realized how stupid he must sound. "I mean—"

"Fabulous observation," Jade said, rolling her eyes. "Here, try one."

Jeremy watched skeptically as she picked up an oyster and spooned red sauce across the top. Then she lifted it up, still in the shell. He really didn't want to eat it, but he decided he better be manly about the whole thing. He held out his hand, but Jade moved the shell out of reach.

"Uh-uh," she said, smiling. "We have to do this right to get the full effect." She leaned across the table and held the oyster above his mouth. "Trust me?" she whispered. Jeremy stared at her and nodded, mesmerized.

"Close your eyes," she commanded.

Jeremy did, and she put the tip of the shell against his lips.

"Now swallow," she instructed.

Jeremy grimaced and almost backed out, but he made himself do it. The silky morsel slipped down his throat and he swallowed, then grinned at her.

"Not bad," he said, wiping his mouth with his linen napkin.

Jade giggled. "See? They're pretty good, huh?"

"Edible," Jeremy cracked.

Jade motioned with her hand. "Okay, my turn." She leaned toward him, her mouth slightly open, and closed her eyes.

Jeremy fed her the same way, making sure his hands were steady as he brought the oyster to her mouth. *Wow*. He'd never thought of eating as *sexy* before.

Apparently there were a lot of things he'd never thought of before he met Jade.

Once the little feeding ritual had ended, an odd silence fell over the table, and Jeremy felt immediately compelled to fill it. There was no way he was going to let one moment of this evening be remembered as boring.

"So, how do you like working at House of Java so far?" he asked, sipping his water.

Jade fingered the clear crystal hanging from a chain around her neck. "It's pretty cool," she answered. "But we've sure got some dorks working there, huh? Like Danny." Jade rolled her eyes. "What's with that greasy-looking baseball cap? Do you think he sleeps with it on or what?"

Jeremy laughed. "I know. I think it's sewn to his head."

"And Corey," Jade continued. "Now, she's missing a couple of brain cells. I swear, if she wasn't Ally's sister, she wouldn't last two minutes as an employee. If she's not out back smoking, she's messing up somebody's order."

Jeremy just nodded. He squirmed a little in his seat. Corey *was* pretty useless at work, but underneath it all, she was okay. And Jeremy had known her forever. He didn't really feel comfortable talking about her.

"And what's Jessica's problem?" Jade paused to take a sip of water. Jeremy could have sworn she was studying him over the rim of her glass.

"I mean, she's kind of a friend and everything," Jade continued, "but she is on a major power trip." She pretended to flip her hair back off her shoulder the way Jessica did. Then she tilted her head to the side and gave him a blank, stupid-looking stare. "Um, Jade?" she said in a high, little-girl squeak. "Could you like lick the floorboards with your tongue? They're like really dirty. I'll be in the back, looking at myself in the mirror, okay?"

Jeremy laughed. He couldn't help it. She'd done a dead-on impression. But his heart felt kind of heavy.

How would he feel if he knew Jessica was out on a date, laughing about him? The thought made his stomach turn.

He stared down at his hands and started twisting his napkin into a roll in his lap. If this was what Jade thought of everybody at work, what did she really think of him? Was she just humoring the local geek by going out on a date with him?

Not that he really wanted to know.

Jade swallowed another oyster, then pushed the empty shell around on her plate. "So, what are we doing after dinner?" she asked.

Jeremy felt his heart skip a beat. He took another swallow of water to stall, but the five extra seconds didn't do him any good. "I have a confession," he mumbled.

She propped her elbows up on the table and rested her chin on her hands. "I *love* confessions."

"I don't think you'll love this kind," Jeremy said.

"Try me."

"Okay." Jeremy took a deep breath. "This dinner is it. This is all I planned." He wasn't about to explain that every single idea he'd come up with seemed totally lame or like he was trying too hard.

Jade grinned a heart-stopping grin. "That's it?"

"That's it," Jeremy said, relaxing slightly.

"Not to worry." Jade smiled wickedly, causing Jeremy's ease to immediately vanish. "I've got a few ideas."

Andy Marsden

<u>To Do This Weekend</u>

1. Creative-writing assignment—one page, using setting to create mood
2. Study for physics test, chapter five
3. Check pool chemicals
4. Clean dog's run
5. Disconnect phone. I'm divorcing all my friends.

CHAPTER
Don't Go There
8

"Excuse me, miss?" A middle-aged man waved at Jessica from a table across the room. "That person with the green hair never brought our espressos."

Jessica wanted to bang her head on the counter. Instead she smiled apologetically. "I'm so sorry. I'll have them right up for you, sir."

She hurriedly scribbled down the next customer's order and scrambled to make their drinks plus the two overdue espressos. As she torqued the handle of the filter basket into the espresso machine, she stared numbly at the crowd filling House of Java. The line for ordering drinks stretched all the way to the front door, and Corey of the green hair, her only help tonight, was out back, smoking a cigarette. As usual.

It was turning out to be exactly the kind of night she'd dreaded when Jade had called in sick that afternoon. Pure chaos. Not only had she not had a chance to sit down for an instant in the last three hours, but she felt like she was running a marathon.

The espressos were finally finished, and Jessica ran around the counter to deliver them. When she stepped back up to the cash register, she almost swore out loud.

Melissa Fox and her little shadow, Cherie, were next in line. Jessica pushed a chunk of damp hair back off her face and tried to smile professionally. "Can I help you?" she asked, her hands folded in front of her.

"I'll have an iced vanilla latte," Melissa said in that cold, demanding voice of hers.

Cherie stepped up next to her friend. "I want a medium chai. And don't make it too hot."

Jessica scribbled down their orders, ignoring their rude tones. "For here or to go?" she asked automatically.

Please let them leave, she prayed.

Melissa smirked at her. "To go. We've got better places to be."

Lucky me, Jessica thought.

While she made their drinks, Jessica could feel the two girls studying her. She sneaked a look at her reflection in the side of the chrome espresso machine. Not good. Her hair was a stringy mess, and her face was all mottled from the heat and exertion. At least her makeup hadn't run down her face—that was something positive anyway.

She placed their cups on the counter and started ringing up the order on the register.

"Tough night, huh?" Melissa asked.

Jessica just shrugged. She knew from experience Melissa didn't chitchat with enemies, and she was still at the top of Melissa's black list. She probably always would be.

Melissa and Cherie shared a catty smile. "I had no idea a person's face could get that red, Jessica," Melissa commented.

"Seriously," Cherie said with a chuckle. "They should make you wear hats here if you're going to sweat so much."

Jessica glared at them, but she kept her mouth shut and took their money. It made her furious to think she'd just made Melissa's night by not having a comeback. That girl liked nothing better than to kick people when they were down. By tomorrow morning she and Cherie would probably have told everybody they knew at Sweet Valley High how butt ugly Jessica Wakefield had looked at House of Java.

Like she really needed that tonight of all nights.

The bells on the front door tinkled again. After hours of nonstop noise they were making her crazy. She eyed the latest knot of people to squeeze in the door. What a bad night for Jeremy to be off. She could use the help.

And the company.

She'd even take Jade this evening. Gladly.

An ugly thought crossed her mind as she stuck a

pitcher of milk under the steam wand. It was kind of odd that Jade had bailed on her the same night Jeremy happened to be off. They couldn't be doing something together, could they?

The thought made her feel like her heart was being squeezed in a vise. Jessica jammed the tip of the steam wand under the surface of the milk and opened the valve.

Don't even go there, she warned herself.

It was only a bad coincidence. She and Jade might have their battles, but not even Jade would ditch her for a date.

Okay, yes, she would, Jessica realized. *In a heartbeat.*

But Jeremy wouldn't. Not even after everything they'd been through. And he was too good a person. He'd never let Jade desert her.

Case closed.

Jessica spooned milk foam on top of the cappuccino. Jade was really sick, and Jessica really needed to get back to work and quit worrying about nothing.

Jade leaned forward and squinted through the windshield of Jeremy's vintage Mercedes. "That's the place," she said. "Park here, behind this van."

Jeremy parked and then leaned forward so he could see around her out the passenger window.

His heart started pounding so hard, he wondered if he was going to have a heart attack. She'd pointed out a piercing-and-tattoo parlor.

112

"What are you going to do to me?" he asked, attempting to sound casual. It came out as more of a squeak.

Jade rolled her eyes and laughed. Hard. "Relax, straight boy," she said when she finally caught her breath. "This is going to be fun."

She turned toward him and gazed into his eyes. "You'd look great with a tattoo, you know," she said quietly, sending chills down his spine.

Not! Jeremy's brain screamed silently. At least one part of his body wasn't affected by her voice.

His hands were starting to sweat, so he shoved them between the backs of his thighs and the leather seat, trying hard to look cool and calm: like the kind of guy who'd been considering having a yin-yang symbol permanently needled into his pecs.

He suspected he was failing miserably.

Proving him right, Jade laughed again. She laid her palm over his pounding heart. "No worries," she said. "We're here for me. This time," she added meaningfully.

"You're getting a tattoo?"

She shook her head. "Belly-button ring. I've always wanted to do it. Tonight just seems like the perfect time." She paused and looked him in the eye. "You've got to do things when they're meant to be, you know?"

A man and a woman walked out of the tattoo place. The guy wore a tight black T-shirt tucked into dirty-looking jeans. The bleached-blond woman with him was much younger. And a lot thinner. The man stopped in front of Jeremy's car. While the woman looked on, he gingerly peeled back the corner of the four-inch square of gauze taped to his forearm.

Jeremy could see a big blot of blood on the bandage. No way he was ever doing that. No way.

"Looks great, babe," the woman said. The man grunted, rolled the bandage back in place, and headed off down the street with his arm around his date.

Jeremy frowned. "Don't you need, like, written permission from your parents or something?"

Jade gave him a pitying look. "You really do need to lighten up." She popped the latch on her seat belt and swung open the car door. "What are they gonna do, have me arrested?" she said as she got out.

Possibly, Jeremy thought.

But Jade was already heading into the shop.

Great, he thought as he locked up his car and followed her. So they'd end the evening with her getting in trouble and him getting killed by her parents when they found out he'd driven her there.

He yanked open the glass door and stepped inside the dark little shop.

"Hi, cutie," a harsh voice squawked practically in his ear. Jeremy jumped about twenty feet and immediately heard Jade laughing.

"He got me too," she said.

Jeremy glanced around for the source of the voice. In the gloom off to his right he finally noticed a wrought-iron cage holding a scarlet parrot.

"*Hasta la vista*, baby," the bird shrieked.

"What a nightmare," Jeremy muttered quietly, shoving his hands into the front pockets of his khakis. The shop looked like something out of a movie—all dank and dirty and filled with smoke.

He and Jade were the only customers in the place, as far as Jeremy could tell. Off to his left two broken-down couches formed an L in the corner under a wall plastered almost to the ceiling with Polaroid photos. They were stuck unevenly all the way to the back of the room, where a partition blocked the rest from view. On the right sat a waist-high counter with an old cash register on it.

The man behind the counter was lifting out a tray from under the glass. He had gray hair pulled back into a scraggly ponytail and granny glasses perched on the end of his nose. He was wearing a long-sleeved shirt rolled up to the elbows under a greasy-looking black leather vest. His forearms were covered with tattoos.

Jeremy shuffled up next to Jade at the counter. She was staring at a velvet tray holding a couple dozen rings, some silver, some gold, some black. Some had colored gems or diamonds in their centers.

"What do you think?" Jade asked him. She pointed

to two of the most delicate-looking gold rings on the tray. "This plain one or the one over there with the ruby?"

Jeremy studied the rings. They were actually sort of cool. He tried to imagine one of them decorating Jade's flat stomach. He swallowed, hard. "I like them both."

Jade shared a look with the guy behind the counter. "Typical male," she commented.

The man snorted.

Jade bit her lower lip. "Okay," she said decisively, "I'll take the one with the ruby."

"You got it," the man said, and picked up the slender ring. He took her money and rang up the sale. "Here's the instructions for how to take care of this; keeping it clean and things." He handed Jade a piece of paper that she folded up and put in her purse.

"You can go stretch out on the table back there," he said, pointing to the partition at the back of the store. "I'll get this in the disinfectant and be right there."

Jade snapped her camera-case purse shut and grinned. Her eyes were twinkling.

"Great," she said calmly, making her way to the back.

Despite the fact that he didn't entirely approve of what she was doing, Jeremy couldn't help but be impressed by how smoothly she was handling the whole thing. Like she'd done this before.

He could hear Jade moving around behind the partition and wasn't sure whether or not she wanted him to go over there. Instead he strolled over to the area by the couches and studied the photos, but he instantly found himself blushing.

He couldn't believe people actually *got* tattoos in places like that, let alone allowed themselves to be photographed. Jeremy turned away, hoping for a safer wall to stare at, but found himself face-to-face with a photo of a triple-pierced cheek. Suddenly the oysters he'd had at dinner weren't sitting too well.

"Hey, straight boy! Come on over here," Jade called out.

Jeremy wasn't exactly sure he wanted to, but he headed back behind the partition anyway. Being with Jade had to be better than being stuck out here.

Jade was lying on a gray Naugahyde table about four feet off the ground. Next to it was a stool. Along the back wall was a sink and a counter covered with bottles of ink and a bunch of wicked-looking instruments.

Jeremy didn't even want to know what they were for.

Jade stretched her arm toward him. "Hold my hand," she commanded. "This is gonna hurt. I need your help."

"Only stings for a minute," the owner said as he walked in.

He snapped on a pair of white latex gloves and

then picked up an instrument that looked like pliers but with wider, flatter tips.

"This is to numb the area," he said, and clamped the jaws around the bottom edge of her navel. He held them there for a minute, obviously increasing the pressure slowly. When he took off the pliers, the area he'd pinched was solid white.

Jeremy stole a glance at Jade's face. She looked completely calm.

Next the man pulled a long, curved needle from a jar of bluish disinfectant. He held it up in front of his face. "Ready?" he asked Jade.

Jade fingered her belly button in the gap between her short shirt and her mini. Then she turned her head toward Jeremy and smiled up at him. She squeezed his hand and stared straight into his eyes.

"Ready," she whispered.

Jeremy covered her hand with both of his. He felt about ten feet tall, knowing she wanted him with her when she did this. No one had ever trusted him like this before.

The next thing he knew, the man had his hands on Jade's bare belly. He swabbed her with a strong-smelling disinfectant, stretched the skin tight, and jabbed the needle right into her.

Jade grunted and scrunched her eyes shut.

A dot of blood appeared where the tip pierced the bottom of her navel.

Jeremy turned his head. For a second he really

wasn't sure his dinner was going to stay down. By the time he was able to look again, the man had removed the needle and was threading Jade's gold ring into the hole.

"All finished," the guy said. "Now, remember to read that sheet on how to take care of this, right?"

"Right," Jade answered, her voice slightly strained.

Jeremy glanced quickly at her. She was smiling up at him, a sheen of tears covering her eyes. Not one fell before she blinked them away. They both looked down at her navel. The tiny gold ring with its miniature ruby was centered at the bottom of her reddened belly button.

"Cool," Jade whispered.

"Definitely," Jeremy agreed.

He was totally impressed, he had to admit. No crying, no screaming, just that tiny little groan.

Jade was one tough girl.

She slipped her hand out from between his and sat up. She stared down at the ring one more time, then she grinned at Jeremy and hopped off the table.

"I feel like celebrating. Let's hit House of Java. I'm definitely in the mood for a triple mocha."

Jeremy bit the inside of his cheek. House of Java? Why would she want to go there when she'd been scheduled to work? He'd assumed she must have come up with some great excuse like a family function or something. And if she showed up there . . .

Finally Jeremy gave himself a mental kick in the

butt. Why would she suggest going to HOJ if she hadn't handled things? She must have found someone to trade shifts.

He took her hand and lifted it toward his lips. "If the lady wants a triple mocha, the lady shall have one," he said, and kissed the back of her hand. "House of Java it is."

The grandfather clock in their living room was just chiming eight when Conner walked through the door. An early night, to be sure, but there hadn't been much going on at the Riot, and Evan had been dragging the whole afternoon, so they decided to call it quits.

Which isn't totally awful, Conner decided as he headed through the empty house to the kitchen. His little sister, Megan, was spending the night at a friend's, and his mother was at some charity ball. She wouldn't be home until late. He had the house to himself for the whole night. He could get a start on his homework and still have time to kick back and watch a little TV.

No responsibilities, no nothing until Monday. Conner wrestled out of his suede jacket and tossed it on the stool next to him.

Then the blinking light on the answering machine caught his eye. Maybe one of his friends from El Carro had come through with a party in the clutch. He pressed the rewind button and grabbed a soda out of the fridge, popping the top. The tape took forever to play back. There had to be a zillion messages. Or at least a couple of long ones.

"Conner, it's Tia. It's about three-thirty. I'm home, studying. I was hoping we could talk."

Conner swallowed a gulp of soda. "Not likely," he commented as the machine moved on to the next message.

"Hey, McD. Andy here. Call me back when you have a sec. Later."

Beep.

"Conner, it's Tia. It's after seven. Please call me back. We really need to talk. Really. I'll be home for—"

He punched the fast-forward button. Anger burned slowly in the pit of his stomach. Why couldn't she just leave him the hell alone?

"Hey, Conner. It's Andy again. Guess you and Evan found something to do after all. I'm desperate to hear your analysis of *The Scarlett Letter*. Just kidding. But really, call me back."

Conner crushed the empty soda can in his hand and played the last message.

"Conner, it's Gavin. I was here, man, but you weren't. Did you *plan* to blow off your guitar lesson today or what? Call me back."

Conner punched the delete button. Great. Nothing like pissing off absolutely everybody in his life.

Oh, well, plenty of time to worry about all that

crap later. Tonight he wasn't going to stress about anybody else. He walked over to the cookie jar and lifted the lid, but two notes on the counter in front of the blender caught his eye.

Conner,
    Check the pool chemicals today. I've asked you twice already. I'm at the Stensons' dinner party. I'll be late.
                    Love, Mom

Conner,

I've got an algebra test on graphing Monday. I don't get this stuff at all! Could you help me go over chapter seven tomorrow? Please?
                    XXXOOO Megan

Conner slammed the top back on the cookie jar, balled the messages up into a tight wad, and launched them across the kitchen. The anger was back full force. He breathed hard, trying to calm his fraying nerves. What was he, Mr. Indispensable all of a sudden? Didn't any of these people realize he had a life too? When the hell was he supposed to do what *he* wanted to do?

Conner clomped up the stairs and down the hall into his room, slamming the door behind him. Three steps across the clothing-strewn floor he stopped, turned on his heel, and went back to the door. He flicked the lock.

Screw the pool and his sister's homework. Screw his lame, needy friends too.

They could all wait.

He sat at his desk and cracked open his calculus book but only managed to finish two problems before his eyes glazed over. Swiveling around in his chair, Conner contemplated the music posters on the wall over his bed. The mirrored doors on his closet were pushed back, so he could see the jumble of clothes inside. The top shelf, where he'd stored stacks of old guitar music, caught his attention. He could just see the edge of the vodka bottle he'd stashed there.

Conner swiveled around to face his desk so quickly, he got a crick in his neck.

No way, he told himself. *Not even a sip.*

He had tons of work to do. And anyway, he'd promised himself he wouldn't have a drop today. He stared hard at his math book, but the numbers swam in front of his eyes in a meaningless jumble. Finally Conner turned around again and stared up at the bottle. What could it hurt anyway? Hell, it might even calm him down—get him focused so he could crank out all that homework.

"Stop it," he told himself, turning back to his homework. He picked up his pencil and started to copy the next problem into his notebook. Halfway through writing out the equation, he gave up and threw the pencil down on his desk.

Pretty soon he found himself spinning in a circle like a ball on a roulette wheel and growing more and more frustrated.

Book. Bottle. Book. Bottle.

There was no telling where he was going to land.

Elizabeth Wakefield

<u>Shopping List</u>
New binder for creative writing—
anything but blue
Two boxes fine-point pens
Pack of ten floppy disks, assorted colors
Bullet-proof heart covering. Just in case.

Jeremy hesitated at the door of House of Java. Just looking through the front window, he realized there was trouble. The place was completely packed. Jessica was racing frantically between the espresso machine and the cash register. She was a total mess. Her face was flushed and sweaty, and she had a panicked look in her eyes.

Jade brushed past him and went inside. Even over the roar of the crowd Jessica obviously heard the bells on the door because she looked straight at Jeremy and Jade.

Her mouth dropped open, and her eyes narrowed. Then her red face got even redder.

If looks could kill, Jeremy figured he and Jade had just been hit with a hydrogen bomb.

This is not good.

He opened his mouth to suggest he and Jade go somewhere else, but she had already gotten in line. There also weren't that many places in Sweet Valley that were open this late.

It doesn't matter that Jessica's mad anyway, Jeremy

reminded himself. *You can date whoever you want to date.*

It seemed like it took forever for them to shuffle their way to the front of the line. Jeremy still hadn't decided what he was going to say to Jessica, but he didn't get the chance anyway.

"Hi, Jess!" Jade said in a perky voice, standing right in front of the cash register. "How's it going?"

"How does it look?" Jessica snapped, sliding a plate of pie down the counter to a waiting customer.

Jade shrugged without even looking around.

"So it's busy. More tips for you!" She leaned over the counter. "I'll have a double mocha with extra whipped cream." She turned to Jeremy. "What do you want?"

Jeremy stepped up to the counter and made himself meet Jessica's furious gaze. At that moment all he wanted to do was run and hide.

"Hey, Jess," he said softly.

She glared back.

Jeremy cleared his throat and shifted his feet. "I'll just have a regular coffee."

Jessica slammed an empty cup down on the counter so he could fill it and looked Jade up and down. "Check out speedy-recovery girl. You look pretty amazing for someone who was so horribly sick a couple of hours ago."

Jeremy almost choked on his own breath. "What?" he said, looking from Jessica to Jade. Jade had called in sick? And then *she'd* decided to bring him here? Was she insane?

To Jeremy's horror, Jade laughed—right in Jessica's face. "What's the big deal?" she asked. "Ally and Mrs. Scott are in San Francisco at that coffee-convention thingy—"

"It's called a trade show," Jessica said.

"Whatever," Jade answered, giving Jessica a long, even look. "Besides, Jess, be honest. I know you must have blown off work for a date at least once in your life."

Jeremy glanced at Jessica, feeling like he'd just been caught cheating or something. She held his gaze for a long moment, and Jeremy knew she was challenging him—daring him to either say something or look away first. Jeremy had never felt such a sharp pang in his heart before.

He finally dropped his chin, wishing he could just disappear. They both knew she'd done it more than once. She'd done it for him.

Ken sighed and pointed the remote at the big-screen TV in the corner of the living room, flicking the station from ESPN to ESPN2. He couldn't stand one more second of NASCAR racing. It reminded him too much of his father.

He grabbed a handful of tortilla chips out of the bag and sat back to watch the tiny girl on the screen jump around on the balance beam.

The TV barely held his attention, though. All he could think about was his father and Faye. They were out together again, doing . . . whatever over-the-hill people did on dates. Apparently Ken's little message-erasing maneuver hadn't done the trick. At that very moment the woman was probably trying to figure out a way to get Ken out of the house perma-nently so she could have more adult alone time with his father.

Unfortunately, all she had to do was wait a few months, until Ken was off at college. By the time he came back for Thanksgiving, she'd probably have his room turned into a walk-in closet.

Just as Ken was working himself into a major at-titude, the doorbell rang. He jumped up, hoping it was Maria or Andy or *anybody* coming to rescue him from his bad mood.

He swung open the door to find Asha standing on the threshold, a paper grocery sack in her arms. What the—

She smiled brightly. "I brought the movies and the ice cream," she said.

"Um . . . ," Ken said brilliantly, still holding on to the doorknob. He automatically took a step back, giving Asha enough room to brush past him into the house. Ken closed the door slowly, racking his brain for something to say.

Asha walked into the living room and then turned to face him, her brow all creased above her nose.

"So where's your dad?" she asked, glancing around the living room as if he were going to pop up from behind the couch and yell, "Surprise!"

"I hope he didn't run out to get dessert or something 'cause I got it all." She held up the bag. "Ice cream, pound cake . . . and I even resisted the chick flicks. You guys can choose between a Schwarzenegger movie and some sort of alien-invasion thing."

"Oh," Ken managed to say. He balled his hands into fists at his sides.

What was he supposed to do? If his father was going to ditch Asha for Faye, the least he could have done was *cancel*. How could he have left Ken to clean up his mess?

He took a long, deep breath. The truth would have to do. Part of it anyway. Ken had never been very good at impromptu lying.

"I'm really sorry, Asha, but, um, my dad's not home right now," he explained, trying to sound casual. Her pretty face fell instantly, and Ken stared down at the tops of his sneakers, unable to make himself meet her eyes.

He heard the crackle of the brown paper as the sack of groceries sagged in her arms.

"I see," she whispered.

Desperate to make her feel better, Ken racked his brain to come up with some sort of plausible story.

"Dad got, um—called out of town to cover a, uh . . . a gymnastics meet. There's a girl from our school who made it to the nationals, and the paper needed him to cover the story at the last minute." He dragged the sole of his shoe back and forth over the carpeting. "He said he was going to call you, but . . . I guess things got hectic or something."

Why am I doing this? he wondered. *Why am I protecting him?*

But when he looked at Asha's hurt and disappointed face, he knew he wasn't lying for his dad. He was lying to protect this sweet, funny, kind woman who his father had dumped all over.

"I'm sorry," Ken said.

Asha dropped the bag of groceries on the magazine-covered coffee table. "You can keep this stuff," she said, forcing a smile. "If I take it home, I'll probably eat it all."

She headed for the door, ducking her head in embarrassment. Ken actually wanted to ask her to stay and watch the movies, but he knew that would be ridiculous. He would just be trying to make them both feel better.

Ken opened the door for her, and Asha paused on the front step. She turned and looked Ken directly in the eye.

"Take care, Ken," she said softly.

"You too," Ken said.

His stomach squeezed in sympathy as he shut the door behind her. He had a feeling she wasn't just saying "take care."

She was saying good-bye.

*   *   *

Once Jessica had made his and Jade's drinks and shoved them across the counter, Jeremy finally risked another glance at her face. She was watching him and looked like she was about to cry. The moment she saw she had his attention, she turned away.

The guilt felt like forty pounds of weight pressing down on his shoulders.

"C'mon, J.," Jade said, tugging at his sleeve. "It's hot in here. Let's grab a table out on the patio."

Without thinking, Jeremy shrugged off Jade's hand. "You go out. I'll be there in a minute," he said, his eyes on Jessica's rigid back.

Jade glanced from Jessica to Jeremy and back again, her face lined with suspicion.

"What?" she said, putting one hand on her tiny hip.

"I said, I'll be out in a minute," Jeremy repeated firmly. Jade blinked with surprise, and Jeremy started to sweat. He didn't want to offend her, but he was confused and even a little angry. He needed a couple of minutes to figure out what to say to her. And he needed to talk to Jessica.

"Fine," Jade said finally. She cast one last look at Jessica, then squared her shoulders and walked off.

Jeremy leaned over the counter and glanced at the growing line behind him. Corey was actually working furiously to get everyone their drinks. She must have realized something was up with Jessica. The girl could be good in a crisis—he had to give her that.

"Hey," Jeremy said, trying to get Jessica to acknowledge him. "Are you gonna be okay?"

"*I'm* not," Corey said, slapping two pieces of cake onto a plate.

"Corey," Jeremy and Jessica both snapped at the same time. She rolled her eyes and rang up her customer.

Jessica finally turned to look at him. "What's the matter?" she said in a sarcastic tone, her eyes rimmed with red that matched her nose perfectly. "Don't I look okay?"

"No, not really," Jeremy answered honestly. She looked like she'd been dragged backward through a keyhole. Not that he'd be stupid enough to say so.

Jessica gestured at the crowd. "I couldn't get anybody to fill in for Jade at the last minute, in case that isn't perfectly obvious." Her blue-green eyes burned with anger. "She called me, like, *five seconds* before her shift, and she was all, '*Jess? I have the worst stomachache. . . .*'"

She pushed her hands through her hair. "I can't even believe I believed her." A quick sigh escaped her lips. "I hope you guys had a good time," she said dryly.

Jeremy almost flinched. He *had* had a good time. Until now. He felt like this whole thing was his fault. He should have canceled the date when he'd found out that Jade had to work tonight. End of story.

Instead he'd been selfish, and now he'd totally imposed on one of his best friends.

At least he hoped that was what Jessica was. At this moment he wasn't so sure.

Jessica took a deep breath and looked past Jeremy, smiling tiredly at the next customer. "What can I get for you?"

Jeremy moved aside slightly and waited for Jessica to finish.

"You need some help," he said when she slammed the cash register shut. "I'm just going to drink my coffee with Jade and drive her home. Then I'll come back and help you close."

Jessica shook her head. "No," she protested, even though he could tell the idea took a load off her mind. "You're on a date. I can handle this. It's not that big—"

"Look, you'll be here all night, cleaning," Jeremy said, cutting her off. "Don't worry about it. I'll be back in a few."

He grabbed his mug and started to wend his way through the crowded café.

"Jeremy!" Jessica called just as he reached the door to the patio. He turned around, balancing his coffee carefully.

Jessica was standing on her tiptoes so that she could see him over the throng of people. "Thanks!" she called.

And then she gave him one of those dazzling

smiles that always hit him right in the pit of the stomach.

Jeremy smiled back, but when he turned again, the smile faded fast.

Now he was going to have to deal with Jade.

"I don't believe it!" Corey blurted out, slumping over the counter.

"I know!" Jessica said. "Hey, that's gross—don't do that," she added, tugging on Corey's black sweater.

Corey groaned but stood up straight again. They both looked over at the front door, which actually hadn't opened—at least not to let anyone *in*—for the past five minutes. Somehow Corey and Jessica had found a rhythm and served the entire line. Now the place was packed with people happily enjoying their drinks, but no one was waiting to order.

Jessica eyed her coworker. "Mind if I . . . ," she said, pointing her thumb over her shoulder at the back room.

"Go ahead," Corey said, slumping again. "But be quick about it. I need a smoke."

"I'll just take five," Jessica promised. Moments later she was flopping onto the lumpy old couch. It felt like every bone in her body was cracking, and her feet were throbbing uncontrollably.

But Jessica barely felt it. All she could do was

smile. Jeremy was cutting his date short to help her. *Her.* This was huge.

"Yes," she exclaimed, raising her fists in the air.

Amazing how the thought energized her. An hour before, she'd been dead on her feet. Now she was practically giddy.

But part of her still couldn't believe she cared. This was Jeremy. She'd given him up long ago.

"A little jealousy goes a long way," Jessica muttered. She wasn't stupid. She knew that it was Jeremy's interest in Jade that had piqued her interest in him again. But she *was* interested. And that was all that mattered.

Jessica sighed and rested her head on the back of the couch, looking up at the ceiling. It had been a long time since she'd been in a little war for a guy's affections. Too long. She'd forgotten how fun it could be. Especially when the guy picked her. Even if she'd won only this one small battle.

Jessica sighed tiredly and stretched her arms up over her head.

It was too weird. Even though it was only jealousy, seeing the concern on Jeremy's face just now had made her remember all his great qualities.

He was definitely kind, and thoughtful, and attentive, and . . . an excellent kisser.

Jessica sat upright. Had Jade and Jeremy kissed yet? The thought made her stomach turn. If they hadn't, they definitely would when he took her home.

Don't think about it, she told herself. There were other details to consider.

Jessica stood, straightened her apron, and headed off to the bathroom to make sure her deodorant was still working. He might be going home with Jade, but he was coming back to her.

And she had no intention of losing the next fight.

Conner McDermott

Creative-Writing Assignment
The haiku is a traditional Japanese verse
form expressing a single emotion or an idea
in which seventeen syllables are arranged in
lines of five, seven, and five syllables.
Create a haiku with an emotional theme.

My Life

Water, rushing black

Shoves me—hard—to the bottom

Never letting up

Jeremy watched Jade spoon a bit of whipped cream off the top of her mocha. She closed her eyes and swallowed, letting out a satisfied little moan. Apparently in the time it took for him to talk to Jessica and get back here, she'd chilled out just a little bit.

But Jeremy couldn't relax with her. He just felt nervous and uncomfortable. They were seated at a small table tucked into the back corner of the patio at House of Java. In the past the tiny white lights strung above the square patio area seemed to twinkle and make the setting romantic. But at the moment Jeremy just wasn't in the mood.

He wished he was, but he wasn't.

Jeremy took a swallow of coffee, then put down the mug and wrapped his fingers around it.

"Jade?" he began. "Can I ask you a question?"

"Feel free," Jade said.

"How could you call in sick on a Friday night?" Jeremy asked, trying to keep the edge out of his voice. "You probably could have found someone to cover your shift."

Jade raised her eyebrows, obviously surprised. "What's the big deal? People do it all the time." She tucked a stray wisp of hair behind her ear. "I mean, just because we have these stupid little jobs that doesn't mean we shouldn't have lives, right?"

"Still." Jeremy frowned at her, shifting in his seat. "Friday's one of our busiest nights."

Jade stared at him blankly for a moment, then dropped her eyes, studying the cup in front of her.

"I know," she said quietly. "But I was so psyched when you asked me out. . . . And I don't know anyone here that well yet. I didn't think anybody would give up a Friday for me." She twirled the little wooden stirrer in her coffee, then picked up the end and licked it. "Besides, who knows when we would have had the same days off?" she added, looking up at him coyly.

Jeremy's heart did a little flip-flop, and his ego started to overpower his conscience. Who knew she wanted to go out with him that much?

Then someone at the next table coughed, and it seemed to bring him back to earth. The fact that they'd had a nice date didn't cancel out the fact that they'd left Jessica in the lurch.

"I was thinking," Jeremy said, leaning forward. "Jessica's really swamped in there. I feel like I should help her out." He took a deep breath, wondering how Jade was going to take this. "I think I should drive you home and come back and help her close."

For a split second he could have sworn Jade

glared at him, but the expression crossed her face so quickly, he easily could have been mistaken.

She bowed her head and then looked up at him through her thick, dark lashes. "But what about the rest of our date?" she asked, sounding almost pouty.

Jeremy smiled slightly. He couldn't help it. She was too cute, even if she had been a little bit thoughtless. "I was hoping we could pick up where we left off another time."

"We could," Jade acknowledged. She looked up at the sky above, then refocused on Jeremy. "But the moon's so gorgeous tonight. I thought we could go to Crescent Beach or something."

Jeremy tightened his grip on his mug slightly. Parking with Jade at Crescent Beach. In the moonlight. He could get into that big time.

But not tonight. He felt way too guilty leaving Jessica like this.

He shook his head. "I'm sorry. Jessica really needs the help."

Jade clucked her tongue, and Jeremy could tell she was about to roll her eyes, but she stopped herself.

"So it's been kind of busy," she said impatiently. "It's not like she hasn't worked on Friday nights before." Jade swirled the last inch of liquid around the bottom of her cup. "By the time you get back, she won't even need the help."

Jeremy almost grinned. It was kind of cool that

she was so irritated about cutting their date short. But he managed to keep a straight face.

"I just don't feel right about leaving her with all this work," he said.

And neither should you, he added silently.

Jade's mouth flattened into a disapproving line. "I don't know what you feel so bad about. You weren't scheduled to work. It wasn't even your problem in the first place."

Exactly, Jeremy thought. *It's yours*. But he had a feeling he knew where all this indignation was coming from. Jade was probably jealous of Jessica. Jealous that he wanted to stay here and help. And he could definitely understand that. Everyone knew he and Jessica had been a couple for a while.

But Jeremy couldn't let this one go. It wasn't right. And Jade should see that.

He toyed with his spoon, twirling it slowly around and around. "Why don't we both stay?" he said without looking up. "We could hang around awhile, help Jessica close up, and then we'd have the rest of the night to—"

"You know what?" Jade said quickly, interrupting him. "My belly button's starting to hurt." She tossed back the last swallow of her drink and slammed down the cup. "Just take me home."

Before he could think of anything to say, Jade stood up, grabbed her purse off the back of her chair, and stalked back into the café.

Jeremy just sat frozen in his seat, watching the doorway. He couldn't believe she'd just stormed out on him like that. All he'd been thinking about for the last week was how he'd never dated a girl like Jade before.

He was beginning to think there was a reason.

After Asha left, Ken stood in the open doorway for a few minutes after her car disappeared around the corner. He felt like a complete jerk. Should he have told her his dad was seeing other women? Didn't Asha deserve the truth?

He closed the door softly and stood in the middle of the living room, staring blankly at the TV. Anger and guilt swirled around inside him. He didn't know how to fix this, and he didn't know why he felt like he had to.

"Maybe because my own father just shoved me into the most awkward situation ever?" Ken muttered.

He switched off the television and headed for his room. He needed advice—clearheaded, intelligent advice. But Maria was at work, and there was no way he could call her there.

Ken sat down on the edge of his bed and stared at the phone. His leg was bouncing up and down, and he was getting increasingly tense by the second. If he didn't vent soon, he was going to end up punching something, and that would be bad. There was really only one person aside from Maria he'd feel comfortable talking about this with.

He picked up the phone and dialed Andy's number.

"Marsden's Bakery," Andy's voice greeted him. "Where butter makes it better."

Ken grimaced. "Hey, Andy. It's Ken."

"Yo," Andy responded unenthusiastically.

"Are you busy?" Ken asked. "I need some advice. Big time."

"Don't we all?" Andy responded, sounding tired.

"Yeah. I guess." Ken picked up a baseball from his bedside table and started to toss it up and down. He felt like if he stopped moving, he was going to explode. Andy had yet to ask him what was wrong, so Ken decided to just keep talking.

"It's my dad," he said finally.

Andy sighed into the phone. "The women thing?" he asked, sounding bored.

Ken's eyebrows scrunched together. He wasn't used to getting such a detached tone from Andy. Had Ken been talking about this enough to annoy his friends?

"Kinda," he said, trying to feel Andy out.

"I suggest you talk to the man," Andy said quickly. "Sometimes simple conversation really helps . . . if you can get any."

Ken nodded. "I know, but I've tried that. He always, like, bites my head off."

"Well, then maybe you should just butt out," Andy said, sounding perturbed. "I mean, it's not really any of your business who your father dates anyway, is it?"

There was a moment of silence in which Ken was wondering whether or not he actually had Andy on the phone and not some psychotic imposter. Ken had never heard the kid snap at anybody before in his life.

"Look, I'm sorry, man," Andy said finally, sounding chagrined. "I didn't mean to snap. I'm just . . . mad at other people, I guess, and I'm taking it out on whoever's around."

Ken leaned forward, resting his elbows on his knees. "You okay?" he asked.

"Yeah," Andy said. "No, actually, but it has nothing to do with you."

"Do you want to talk about it?" Ken asked, starting to get concerned. Then Andy laughed. Long, loud, and hard. "What's funny?" Ken asked, totally confused.

"I just can't believe you asked me that," Andy said, catching his breath. "You are the only person who's asked me that in, like, two weeks, and I just can't believe it."

Ken raised his eyebrows. "Well, do you want to?"

"No, that's all right," Andy said slowly. "Eventually, yeah, but there are some other people I have to talk to first."

"All right. Let me know," Ken said, throwing the ball again.

"I will," Andy said, sounding a lot less stressed than he had one minute ago. "And you just talk to your dad. Make him listen to you. Do whatever it takes."

Ken missed the ball, and it slammed down on his bedpost, ricocheted across the room, and knocked down one of the photographs on his wall. It fell to the floor, the glass shattering and the frame bending in half.

"You okay?" Andy asked at the sound of the crash.

"Yeah," Ken said, staring at the mess. "I'll talk to my dad if you talk to . . . whoever you need to talk to."

Andy laughed. "Sounds like a plan."

After he hung up the phone, Ken went over and picked up the framed picture of his Little League baseball team. His dad, who was his coach at the time, was standing there beaming, with his hand on Ken's shoulder. Back then, he'd felt like he could talk to his dad about anything.

Now the photo was ruined, just like his relationship with his father. Ken turned and shoved the frame into the garbage can.

Maybe it was time to start over. If he could just get a little bit of that feeling back, maybe everything would be okay.

*   *   *

Focus on the good parts of the night, Jeremy told himself as he drove Jade home. *There were definite good parts. Just focus on those.*

But even as he pep talked himself to death, Jeremy could feel the tension growing in the car. She hadn't said a word to him since they left House of Java. They were only a couple of blocks from her house when he finally risked a glance in her direction.

In the darkened car he couldn't read her expression at all, but he had a feeling she was studying him too.

He hit the brakes at a stop sign under a streetlight and turned to her. "So, is your belly button okay?" he asked.

Jade kept her eyes straight ahead. She barely nodded in acknowledgment.

Jeremy sighed. He didn't know what else to do. If she wanted to pout all the way home, it seemed he was just going to have to let her.

The rest of the drive to her house seemed to take forever. Once he pulled into her driveway, he put on the parking brake but kept the motor running. Part of him felt obligated to get out and walk her to the door, but it was a very small part that didn't win out.

The light from her front porch flooded the car. When she didn't immediately throw off her seat belt and jump out of the car, Jeremy turned toward her, puzzled.

She smiled at him, a little uncertainly. "I'm sorry I didn't offer to stay and help Jessica," she said softly. "I know I should have, but my belly button really hurts. I guess it's kind of getting to me. I shouldn't have made you bring me home first. I'm sorry."

"That's okay," Jeremy said automatically. It was pretty much what he always said when someone apologized for anything.

"Anyway, I really want to do this again," Jade said, unbuckling her seat belt. She turned and put her hand on his knee lightly. "I mean, the fun-date part, not the getting-stabbed-in-the-stomach-and-making-a-scene-at-House-of-Java part."

Jeremy snorted a laugh, feeling a lot more comfortable now that she was talking. Of course the hand on his leg was distracting enough to kill his powers of speech.

"I had a really good time," Jade said.

"Me too," Jeremy answered, finally finding his voice. "On the fun-date part," he added.

She looked down and touched the skin around her belly-button ring. "I'm really glad you were with me when I got this," she said. "Kind of an unforgettable first date."

Jeremy couldn't stop staring at the gold ring with its tiny, bloodred ruby. "I know *I'll* never forget it."

His words hung in the air for a minute, and the silence ate away at Jeremy's nerves. He toyed with the keys dangling from the ignition. What exactly was he supposed to do now? With Jade it was pretty damn hard for a guy to tell.

Then out of nowhere he felt her fingers touch his chin, and she gently turned his head so he was facing her again.

"So are you going to kiss me or what?" she asked.

Jeremy's heart plummeted directly through his body. He started to say something, but she cut him off, which was good since he had no idea what he was about to say.

"Okay, if you won't, I will," Jade said. She leaned across the gearshift toward him, her fingers still touching his face, her other warm hand pressed into his thigh. Jeremy closed his eyes, and suddenly her lips were touching his.

It was a slow, searching, sweet kiss, and it seemed to last forever. Jade's hand moved to the back of his neck, and she pulled him into her lightly, sending chills down Jeremy's spine.

He'd certainly been kissed before, but never like this.

Not even close.

Then in an instant Jade pulled back. Before Jeremy's clouded mind could react, she had popped open the passenger door and climbed out.

"Night," she said. She took off toward the front door without waiting for him to reply.

Jeremy watched until she was safely inside, unsure of whether he even had the brainpower to drive.

He felt like that kiss had sapped his energy and left him useless. Happy, but useless.

Finally he started to back out of the drive. His lips were still tingling, along with the rest of his body.

Jeremy suddenly had the feeling he was going to have no trouble focusing on the good parts.

Conner had just dropped into the zone where he was nicely buzzed, nodding to some thrashing guitar riffs, when the doorbell shattered his mood as thoroughly as a hammer smashing glass.

"Damn," he yelled over the thumping music that filled his room.

He stalked through the empty house to the front door, hoping it was just Megan and she'd forgotten her keys. Anyone else was going to get a serious dose of attitude.

He swung open the door and groaned.

It was Tia.

"Nice greeting," she said, her arms crossed over her chest.

Conner reached up, rested his hand on top of the door, and just looked at her. He was not in the mood. Of course, Tia didn't pick up on his go-away vibes.

"What's wrong with you?" she spat, glaring up at him. "Don't you ever listen to your messages? Why didn't you call me back?"

"Back off, Tee," Conner snapped back, rage flaring instantly inside him. Fueled by alcohol, it ran down his nerve endings like a spark running down a fuse. "I'm not your slave. I don't owe you anything." He clenched his hands into fists. "I've got a right to privacy, you know. Maybe to a little time to myself." He slammed the door in her face and stalked back upstairs to his room.

Couldn't the girl take a hint? Conner wasn't interested in hooking up with her anymore. And she had repeatedly refused to talk to him on a friendship level. Now, because it was convenient for her, he was supposed to just be at her beck and call?

Hardly.

Conner slammed his bedroom door, and an instant later it was flung open again. Tia stalked in, shoulders rolled back, lips pursed.

"What's your problem?" she demanded, standing in the center of his room. Conner had to hand it to her—he'd never known Tia to back down from a confrontation.

He rolled his eyes and switched off the stereo.

"You know what, Tee? Fine. Say what you came to say." He leaned back in his desk chair and thrust his legs out in front of him, crossing them at the ankles. Maybe if he heard her out, she would go away.

Tia pushed her long, dark hair back away from her face and blew out a huge breath.

"I hate this, Conner," she said, wrapping her arms

around her petite frame. "I hate being like this with you." Her face was scrunched up like she was trying not to cry. "There's never been anything that we couldn't talk about, and now it's like you're always hiding from me."

Conner blinked. He wasn't *hiding;* he just wanted to be alone. There was a difference. Kind of.

Tia bit her lower lip. "Anyway, I came here to tell you . . . I came here to tell you that we can't fool around anymore. I mean, I know it sounds weird, but I don't want to hurt Liz, and I think that we . . . I really think that we'd be better off staying friends." She looked at him, half scared, half hopeful. "If that's even possible."

"Wait a minute," Conner said, leaning forward in his chair. "Are you trying to tell me that you're here to *dump* me?"

Tia's eyes narrowed slightly. "I never said—"

"Because if you are, you need to get a serious clue," Conner said. "You can't dump what you never had."

Tia's head pulled back as if she'd been slapped, and her face drained of color. "How could you—"

"God, Tia! So we hooked up a few times, so what?" Conner asked, pushing himself to his feet. A monster head rush overtook him, and Tia blurred in front of his eyes. He almost lost his balance, which just made him even more angry. Why did everybody have to push him so hard? Tia, his mother, even

Elizabeth . . . He felt like they were squeezing the life out of him.

"I mean, you act like you're breaking up with me," Conner said, pressing his hands into the edge of the desk until he felt it cutting into his palms. "What did you think? Did you think I was going to dump Liz for you or something? Are you nuts?"

"No," Tia choked out. "I didn't think you were going to—"

"Because I wasn't," Conner continued. "I never was. I'm not even attracted to you."

Tia pressed both her hands into her middle as if he'd just punched her in the gut. Her tears spilled over then, but for some reason her pain only made him madder. It was more pressure. More for him to fix.

"I can't believe you're talking to me like this," Tia said through her tears. "I thought we were friends. I thought you cared about me."

Conner studied her. Saw her pale face streaked with tears and her puffy, red lips. *You do care about her, you idiot!* his brain screamed. *What the hell are you doing?*

But it was like someone else was in charge of his mouth—someone who had no connection to his brain.

"Whatever," Conner said, looking pointedly away from her tears. "I just wish you'd leave me the hell alone."

"Fine," Tia said finally, taking a deep breath and quickly wiping both cheeks with the backs of her hands. She started to storm out of the room, but she froze halfway to the door.

Conner glanced over at her. She was staring at the nearly empty vodka bottle on top of his math book.

Damn.

Tia looked up at him, her eyes wide and confused. "Conner, what—"

There was no way she was finishing that sentence. He lurched forward, grabbed her by the upper arm, and shoved her out of his room. "Go home, Tia," he shouted. "Just get the hell out of here."

He slammed his bedroom door behind her, grabbed the bottle, and flung it into the opposite wall, where it shattered with a satisfyingly loud crash. Then he saw that a few drops of liquid were trickling down the wall, and it hit him like a ton of bricks.

That was the last of his stash.

Elizabeth Wakefield

From: lizw@cal.rr.com
To: tee@swiftnet.com
Time: 8:47 p.m.
Subject: Shopping

Hey, Tee—
  I know things have been completely bizarre lately, so I figured we should do what we do best. Shop.
  Want to hit the mall tomorrow? I'm dying to wear those new khakis I bought at Old Navy, but I don't have any shoes.
  Maybe Conner could meet us at the food court for lunch. If it's not too weird.

                              Love, Liz

TIA RAMIREZ

From: tee@swiftnet.com
To: lizw@cal.rr.com
Time: 9:53 p.m.
Subject: re: Shopping

hi back—
   i'd love to go, but this weekend
isn't good.
   sorry—
                        love, tia

When Jeremy got back to House of Java, the only customer left was a college-age guy packing up his laptop. Jeremy was still half out of it from that outrageous kiss as he breezed through the door. Even so, he noticed Jessica's face light up.

"Thanks for coming back," she said as soon as he'd reached the front counter. She looked a lot better. Somehow she'd found the time to brush out her hair and put on a little lip gloss. It was almost as if the whole crazy night had never happened.

"No problem," Jeremy said with a shrug. Suddenly being here seemed kind of silly. Now that the place was dead, it wouldn't take her *that* much longer to clean up. Jeremy brushed the thought aside and started moving some of the lighter furniture against the walls so he could sweep up. The place was still a wreck. He was glad he was here. Really.

"Where's Corey?" Jeremy asked.

"She bailed, of course," Jessica answered. "She said she wasn't scheduled to close, so . . ."

"Nice of her," Jeremy said sarcastically.

Jessica came out from behind the counter and picked up a few dirty napkins left on one of the tables.

"Well, I expect it from Corey, but can you believe Jade?" she asked. "I mean, call in sick and then show up to rub it in my face? That is so totally rude."

Jeremy calmly continued to work. The college guy stepped around him and headed out the door.

"Don't you think that's rude?" Jessica insisted, tossing the napkins into a garbage can.

Jeremy shook out a velvet pillow that had hit the floor and replaced it on its chair. "Not my department, senorita," he said in a bad, fake accent.

Jessica moved around the table in front of him until she was facing him. He was forced to meet her gaze. "You don't think she was completely out of line?" she asked.

Jeremy's shoulders sagged. He sighed. "Look, I came back to help because you looked like you needed a hand. Whatever Jade did, she's going to have to deal with on her own."

"But—," Jessica said, but then seemed to think the better of it. Her blue-green eyes clouded with confusion for a moment. Then she blinked and gave him a small smile. "You're right. I guess I'll just talk to her about it next week."

Jeremy didn't reply. What made Jessica think he'd gossip about the girl he was dating anyway?

She knows me better than that, he thought as he headed for the closet to get the broom.

As he started working, he watched her wipe down the front counter. Even from across the room he could see the exhaustion in her face. Jeremy immediately felt guilty again. She'd had a seriously bad day. He had to cut her some slack.

With two of them working, it took less than an hour to clean up. While Jeremy waited by the front door, Jessica hurried to the back to leave her apron and grab her purse.

"Thanks for the help," she said, putting on her jacket as she rounded the counter and walked over to him. "It was really nice of you."

Jeremy shrugged. He was feeling kind of tired now himself, and he was ready to blow this pop stand. "It's not like I don't do it every other night. No big deal."

"Yeah, it is," Jessica said, smiling up at him.

"Okay, you're right," Jeremy said finally. "I'm a pretty cool guy."

"I wouldn't say *that,*" Jessica said. Jeremy laughed, but then Jessica reached up and circled her arms around his neck, grabbing him in a quick hug. It took him by surprise, and for a moment he forgot to breathe. Then, feeling awkward, Jeremy circled her waist with his arms and hugged her back lightly.

He expected her to let go quickly. After all, this

was a friendly thank-you hug, right? But she didn't. She rested her cheek against his chest. The top of her head fit right below his chin, just the way he remembered.

"Uh, Jess—"

She tilted back her head until their eyes met. "Why did I ever break up with you?" she asked softly.

The look in her eyes made his stomach drop. She was going to kiss him.

Oh God.

Jeremy panicked. He stiffened, then reached back and gently took her wrists and pulled them away from his neck. "Jess, don't."

As he watched, her expression changed from embarrassment to anger and finally hurt. It hardly took an instant.

She took a step back and started to fumble with her purse. Her hair fell forward, hiding her expression from him.

Jeremy felt like he'd slapped her. "I—I'm sorry," he stammered. He started to reach out to her and then thought better of it, jamming his hands into his pants pockets. "I'm sorry. When I said I'd come back and help, I didn't mean to . . . to give you the wrong idea." He paused as she abruptly stopped her frantic search for whatever she was looking for. "I just came back to help out a friend," he finished softly.

Jessica finally lifted her eyes, letting her pocketbook

drop to her side. A tiny smile tugged at the corner of her mouth.

"Don't apologize. I'm the one who should be sorry." She tried to laugh, but it came out more like a croak.

"Jess—"

"I guess I just got caught up in the romance of the moment," she joked, laughing tightly as she pulled her keys out of her jacket pocket. "You know how sentimental I get about closing up together."

Before he could think of anything to say, she was out the door. Jeremy smiled sadly and shook his head, feeling heavy and tired. Leave it to Jessica to find a way to laugh it off. He dug the keys to the shop out of his pocket, switched off the lights, and stepped out into the cool night air.

It hit him as he locked the door. He'd just told Jessica Wakefield flat out that he only wanted to be friends, and he was calm about it. Completely calm.

And completely certain.

For the first time he was completely, utterly, absolutely certain. He and Jessica. Just friends.

Ken was in the living room, watching SportsCenter, when he heard the key turn in the front-door lock. He moved to the edge of the couch, ready to jump up and escape to his room if his dad had brought Faye with him.

The door swung open, and his dad was alone.

For once. Ken relaxed back against the couch.

"Hi, Dad," he said.

"Hi," his dad replied. He took off his sport coat, tossed it on the arm of the couch, and flopped down across from Ken.

That was it. Conversation over.

All through the hockey report Ken tried to think of how to say what he wanted to say. After practicing a few opening lines in his head, he realized there was no good way to begin. Once the commercials came on, he punched the power button on the remote.

"Listen—"

Before he got any further, his father grabbed the remote off the coffee table and switched the TV back on.

"What'd you do that for?" he asked irritably.

"Dad, I was wondering if we could talk," Ken said over the sound track of a tire commercial.

SportsCenter came back on. His father held up his hand. "Hang on. I want to hear the basketball scores."

Ken pressed his lips together tightly. *That's my dad— sports before eating or breathing. Definitely before me.*

Determined to have it out, Ken scooted forward on the couch until he could rest his elbows on his knees.

You can do this, he told himself. *It's just Dad.*

He laced his fingers together and squeezed, causing his knuckles to turn white.

"Dad," he began again, "I need to talk to you about Asha."

He glanced at his father from the corner of his eye to gauge his reaction. But there didn't seem to be one. His dad was staring straight ahead at the TV, his mouth set in a tight line. Ken could see the shifting images reflecting in his eyes.

He took a deep, calming breath. *One word at a time. Just keep the ball moving.*

He cleared his throat and plunged on. "She came by tonight. You stood her up, and I had to make some lame excuse. But she knew." He stopped again, waiting for some kind of sign that his father was even listening to him, but the only change Ken could detect was a tightening of the muscles in his father's jaw.

Ken doubted he could have moved an inch, his body was so tense. The knots in his stomach were so bad, he thought he was going to throw up. He swallowed hard.

"I just want to know why you're doing this," he blurted out. "Asha's really cool, and it's like . . . you're just jerking her around. Like a kid or something."

An instant later Ken knew he'd gone too far. His father turned to face him, and Ken could practically see steam coming out of his ears like in an old-fashioned cartoon. The man was fuming.

"What the *hell* makes you think you have the right to question me?" he shouted, standing up so

165

that he towered over Ken. "I don't want to hear one more word from you."

"But Dad, I—"

"*You're* calling *me* a kid?" his father interrupted him, crossing his beefy arms over his chest. "What about you, Ken? I don't know where you think you get off, preaching maturity to me."

Ken had no idea what to say, and even if he did, he probably couldn't have spoken past the lump in his throat.

"Did I or did I not ask you last night if there were any messages for me?" Ken's father spat.

There was no air in Ken's lungs. He was dead. Totally dead.

"I knew it," his father said, reading Ken's guilty expression. He took a couple of steps back, shaking his head. "You know exactly what I'm talking about. You did erase that message from Faye."

"Dad . . ." It was nothing but a whisper.

"Nice one, Ken. You're lucky she caught me at work. Didn't think that far ahead, did you, Mr. Mature?"

Ken rubbed his hand over his face. He couldn't look his father in the eye. "Okay, I shouldn't have—"

"You're damn right you shouldn't have," his father shouted.

"Dad, I'm sorry, but I just think—"

His father grimaced in disgust. "You don't think at all." He laughed. "What makes you think I'm going to take advice from a kid who's blown his own future so badly, he couldn't find the pieces with a microscope?"

Ken couldn't breathe. He felt like he'd just taken a block to the gut. "What are you talking about?"

His dad ran a hand through his short hair. Then he glared at Ken with a lot more than anger in his eyes. It almost looked like hatred.

"How do you think it feels to write about all those kids winning games, breaking records, and knowing it should have been my kid?" his father said. "Except my kid's a coward who threw his future right down the frigging toilet."

Ken just stared at his father in disbelief.

"My son, the backup quarterback." He let out a sarcastic laugh. "You might as well be the damned equipment boy. So don't lecture me on life, Ken. You've got nothing to say."

With that, his father grabbed the remote and sat down in the armchair next to the couch, shutting Ken out completely.

Ken couldn't move. His legs were shaking so badly, he didn't think they'd hold his weight. He sat there, three feet away from his father, waiting for him to say he was sorry, that he hadn't meant to say all those horrible things. But his dad simply stared at the talking heads behind the sports desk as if he hadn't just shattered his son's heart.

When he finally thought he could stand, Ken

slowly rose to his feet and shuffled down the hall to his room. He shut the door quietly and lay facedown on his bed, feeling like every bone in his body had been broken. Gingerly he turned his head to the side, resting his cheek on the rough plaid bedspread. The corner of the picture he'd broken stuck out of the top of the trash can by his desk. Hot tears stung his eyes and then ran down his cheeks. He squeezed his eyes shut against the pain.

I get it, Dad, he thought. *If I'm not the best, I'm nothing.*

Jessica drove the Jeep away from House of Java, and for the first three blocks she was perfectly fine. She felt this weird numbness in her heart, yet she was hyperalert to everything around her—the deserted street, the bright, clear colors of the stoplights against the black night sky, the hum of the Jeep's tires on the pavement.

Everything was fine. Really, really fine.

Then reality hit. Jeremy had rejected her. Rejected her. And before she knew what was happening, the tears started. She tried wiping them away as she drove, but before another block passed, she couldn't see a thing. She yanked the wheel to the right and pulled to the curb.

She'd been rejected. Dissed. Dumped. Passed over for Jade. It was humiliating, mortifying, painful. She gave up trying to stop the tears. It was useless.

"This is not happening," she whispered between sobs. "Jeremy did not just turn me down."

But the scene at House of Java wouldn't stop replaying over and over in her head like some horrible video clip. Her throwing her arms around Jeremy's neck. Leaning in for a kiss. Being pushed away. *Pushed* away. Jessica was pretty sure that had never happened to her before.

And Jeremy was the one who had done it. Sweet, kind, caring Jeremy who wouldn't hurt a fly. Who was supposed to be in love with her.

Her. Not Jade. How could that just go away? But there was no answer to that question, so Jessica just draped herself over the steering wheel and cried.

My life completely sucks, Andy thought as he circled the HOJ parking lot for the third time, trying to find a space big enough for his boat of a Cadillac. Was the entire world addicted to coffee?

Okay, so it *was* Saturday morning. What had he expected? He finally saw a spot he'd overlooked the first two times and inched his humongous car into it.

Please, he prayed, *don't let there be anybody I know here. Not yet.*

Andy wasn't in the mood to hang with his friends and be ignored as usual, but he couldn't stand staring at the walls of his room another second either. Studying at House of Java seemed like the perfect solution. At least it would be a change of scenery. He grabbed his backpack, locked the car, and headed into the café.

Antisocial didn't come close to describing how he felt this morning. After talking to Ken the night before, Andy had felt better. He'd felt ready to grab Tia or Conner and make them listen to him, but the more he thought about it, the less confident he became. There was no way he was going to get anyone to talk to him about him until all their own drama died down. And lately it seemed like that was never going to happen.

He was sick of being Andy the Adviser, Andy the Clown, Andy the Guy with No Problems. His so-called friends had rubbed his nerves raw.

The instant he opened the door, Andy spotted Jessica behind the counter. He tried to sneak around the edge of the room to a secluded booth, but she saw him and waved.

Andy waved back unenthusiastically and slid into the booth. He'd only just opened his physics book when Jessica set a blue glass mug topped with foamed milk in front of him.

"Your usual. Double caramel cap, right?" she asked.

Andy nodded. "Right, thanks."

Up close, he could tell she didn't look too hot. Well, as not as hot as Jessica Wakefield was capable of looking anyway. Her sweater and jeans were, of course, right out of the pages of *Seventeen,* and her gleaming blond hair was tucked neatly behind her ears. But there were dark circles under her eyes, and she actually looked sort of vulnerable. Something he hadn't seen in Jessica in a while, for sure.

She slid into the seat across from him. "I'm on my break. Is it okay if I join you?" she asked in a small voice.

He sighed and closed his physics book. "What's up?" he made himself ask.

Jessica smiled with relief. "You would not believe what happened last night."

"No, I probably—"

"Jade's been horrible to me since she started working here," Jessica continued.

Andy rested his chin on his palm and stared up at the ceiling while he stirred his cappuccino with his other hand. He clearly wasn't going to get a word in. Not that he wanted to anyway.

"She's totally obnoxious and rude every time I ask her to do anything. And that's not even the worst part." She paused dramatically. "Jeremy actually asked her out."

Andy took a sip of his drink. He pushed one corner of his physics book around and around until the whole book was spinning in place. How long was Jessica's break anyway?

"And then she called in sick to go out with him," Jessica went on incredulously. "Can you even—"

A shadow crossed the table. "Oh, give it up, Jess," Maria cut in. "You dumped him, remember?"

Before Andy could say hello, Maria had plopped her butt onto the bench next to him and shoved her hip into his. "Scoot over," she ordered.

Being considerably smaller, Andy figured he didn't have much choice.

"Ma'am, yes, ma'am," he said sarcastically, sliding as far into the booth as he could.

Maria eyed Andy up and down. "That's more like it." She laced her fingers together on top of the table and glanced from Andy to Jessica.

"I'm really worried about Ken," she announced.

Shocker, Andy thought, trying hard not to roll his eyes.

Jessica leaned forward, her brow creased with concern. "What happened?"

"He and his dad had a big fight last night about his dad's girlfriends," Maria explained. "Ken wouldn't tell me exactly what his dad said, but he's like zombie boy this morning. He wouldn't even come out for pancakes."

"That is big," Jessica said.

Andy flipped his textbook open and shut, trying to ignore them. He was so sick of hearing about everyone else's problems. And he felt guilty about being sick of it. The whole thing just made him tense.

"What do you think he's going to do?" Jessica was saying the next time he tuned in.

Maria was playing with a packet of sugar, standing it end over end. "I have no idea. I'm thinking—"

"Hey, guys." Elizabeth scooted into the booth next to Jessica and took a sip from a small bottle of water.

"Why don't you join us?" Andy muttered sarcastically. He was pretty sure none of the girls even heard him.

Maria frowned at Elizabeth. "You don't look so good. What's up?"

"What did the idiot do now?" Jessica asked, narrowing her eyes.

The idiot was Jessica-speak for Conner.

Andy sighed and swirled the foam in the bottom of his mug.

"It's not him." Elizabeth shook her head. "It's Tia. I mean, I'm trying to be friends with her, which I think is pretty cool of me. *She's* the one who—"

"Attacked your boyfriend?" Maria interrupted her.

"I'd never talk to her again if I were you," Jessica added.

Andy shifted uncomfortably in his seat. This was getting a little out of line.

Elizabeth nodded miserably. "I know, but I'm not you, Jess. I mean, I invited her to go shopping today, and she wrote me this cryptic message, turning me down. Like she was busy all weekend. What's that all about?"

"Maybe you should—," Maria started to say.

"Forget about it and—," Jessica said at the same time.

Andy stared at the oil painting of the big, round woman sipping coffee, making his eyes focus and then unfocus until the painting was just a blur of colors. He was trying to pretend he wasn't even there, but it wasn't working very well. As the girls talked, their voices kept getting louder and louder until he wanted to scream at them to shut up.

Couldn't they stop talking about themselves for five seconds? Didn't it occur to anyone that maybe he'd come here alone so that he could *be* alone?

". . . and why are you so hung up on Jeremy anyway?" Maria's voice invaded Andy's head.

Jessica sighed. "I know. It's stupid, but . . ."

Andy screwed his eyes shut and covered his ears with his hands, trying to block them out completely. Conner, Jeremy, Jade, Tia, Ken, the evil Mr. Matthews. Were these really *problems?* At the moment Andy didn't think so.

Worrying about how to tell your ex-girlfriend that you think you want to date her brother. *That* was a problem.

"So what do you think I should do?" Elizabeth or maybe Jessica asked.

"Maybe you should talk—"

"I know. How about—"

174

The girls were all talking so fast, they were tripping over each other. Andy couldn't take it for another second. His tension level was sky-high.

He cleared his throat loudly. "Hey, um, you guys, could you quiet down?"

"Yeah, but what if Ken—," Maria said right over the top of him.

"You just have to—"

"Hey," Andy yelled. "Would you guys *shut up?*"

They ignored him.

He grabbed the spoon out of Jessica's hand and banged it against the side of his mug.

Nothing. He might as well have been invisible. He couldn't take it anymore. He just couldn't—

"So, you guys," he said in a normal voice. His friends continued to talk.

"And then he said—"

"I never thought—"

"If she would only—"

"I think I might be gay."

Maria dropped her spoon. Elizabeth's hand hit the table and knocked over her bottle of water. Jessica didn't move. In fact, no one moved for a good ten seconds.

Except Andy. Andy smiled like he'd never smiled before.

Silence.

Finally.

ANDY MARSDEN

11:04 A.M.

So now I've got their attention. Question is, do I really want it?

TIA RAMIREZ
11:10 A.M.

I CAN'T BELIEVE CONNER'S
DRINKING. I MEAN, HE'S ALWAYS
BEEN A DRINKER AT PARTIES
AND STUFF, BUT NOT A <u>DRINKER.</u>
THIS IS BIG. MEGABIG. I MEAN,
HE'S SUCH AN IDIOT. HOW COULD
HE DO THIS AFTER EVERYTHING HE
WENT THROUGH WITH HIS
MOTHER? HOW COULD HE DO
THIS TO MEGAN? HOW COULD HE
DO THIS TO LIZ?

HOW COULD HE DO THIS TO
ME?

I HAVE TO TALK TO ANDY.

JADE WU
12:15 P.M.

Jeremy just called to tell me what a nice time he had last night. Jessica probably thought she won some kind of battle or something when he said he'd come back and help her scrub the floors or whatever. (Ick, by the way.) But I knew that kiss would put me over the top.

It always does.

CONNER MCDERMOTT

1:07 P.M.

My head hurts.

My back hurts.

My eyes hurt.

And my mom is yelling something about pool chemicals.

Someone just shoot me now.